SPEED DATING

a **DATING GAME** novel by Natalie Standiford

 LITTLE, BROWN AND COMPANY

New York ⌁ Boston ⌁ London

For Julie Roth Jolson, Emily Uhry,
and Gail Herman

1 Chocolate Brainwash

HERE IS TODAY'S HOROSCOPE: CAPRICORN: Cheer up! Your suffering will end soon. Then it will come back. Then it will go away again . . . and come back again. . . .

Holly Anderson pressed an icy wash cloth over her eyes—her mother's never-fail de-puffing trick. When the doorbell rang she quickly stashed the cloth in the freezer. Lina and Mads had arrived to cheer her up. Even though they were her best friends, Holly didn't like to look as if she'd been crying.

Madison Markowitz and Lina Ozu trooped in with grocery bags full of post-breakup supplies.

"That dirty little punk," Mads said.

"He's not exactly little," Holly said. They were talking about Rob Safran, Holly's boyfriend—*ex*-boyfriend—who was tall and swim-team-muscular. Heart-meltingly so.

"Okay," Mads said. "That big, weird-haired dork. With Frankenstein feet. I always thought his hair looked like it was sewn onto his scalp."

"*Now* you tell me," Holly said. Rob's hair was so thick, it looked like teddy bear fur. Unlike Mads (news to Holly), Holly had always loved his hair. Uh-oh . . . tears coming on. Holly pinched her forearm to suppress them. Once they started coming, they were hard to stop.

"We're sympathy-trashing him," Lina said. "For your sake. Doesn't it make you feel better?"

"Not really," Holly said.

"You should go online and X-Rate him right now," Mads said. "Really give it to him, so no girl will want to come within five miles of him. He won't get another girl-friend until college!"

"That's abusing the system," Holly said. Not that she hadn't been tempted. X-Rating was a feature on the girls' Web blog, the Dating Game, where kids from their school rated their ex-boyfriends and ex-girlfriends. "And, any-way, Rob doesn't deserve it. I don't think. I haven't quite sorted out my feelings yet."

She caught a glimpse of herself in the shiny aluminum lid of a pot. The lid distorted her features, but even correcting for that, she looked terrible. Her big blue eyes were still red and puffy, in spite of her mother's trick, and her long blond hair was matted and tangled. Mads and Lina had to have noticed she was upset. She pushed the lid away.

Mads reached into a shopping bag and pulled out three pints of ice cream. "Let's get down to business. We've got Strawberry-Banana Happiness-in-a-Tub, Mint-Chocolate Love-Substitute, and Intense Chocolate Brainwash, to chocolatize your troubles away."

"These ice-cream names are really getting out of hand," Holly said. "I mean, we all know what ice cream is for. Do they have to spell it out?"

Lina plopped her grocery bag on Holly's kitchen island. "I've got cheese popcorn, Cheez Doodles, and Wheat Thins, in case you get a salt jones," she said.

"I'll start with the hard stuff," Holly said, reaching for the Chocolate Brainwash. "Thanks for coming over, you guys. I was almost on the verge of tears there, for a minute."

"The *verge* of tears?" Mads picked up a soggy pile of used Kleenex and tossed it in the trash.

"You heard me." Holly was playing the tough guy, though she knew Mads and Lina saw through it.

"I still can't believe he dumped you," Lina said. "After all you went through with him! After he begged you to be in his sister's wedding—"

"—and she made you wear that heinous bridesmaid's dress—" Mads said.

"—and you practically planned the whole thing for her," Lina said.

"Not to mention all the swim meets you went to," Mads said. "We *all* went to. Screaming for him like a bunch of cheer-bots."

"Rob should be shunned for this," Lina said. "Ostracized from the community. Like the Amish do when somebody breaks the rules."

"It's not that bad," Holly said. "He has his reasons."

"Like what?" Lina asked.

"Well, he said he was so busy with swimming—"

"Lame."

"—and school—"

"Lame."

"—and studying for the SATs—"

"Totally lame."

"—and dealing with his parents' divorce—"

"Please."

"—that he doesn't have time to be in a relationship right now," Holly finished.

"Yeah? Well, who doesn't have to deal with school and activities and parental insanity?" Mads said. "We're all busy."

"You have to make time for love," Lina said.

"Well, that's what he told me," Holly said. "He said, 'You're a cool girl, I'm really into you, we've had fun, but I don't think I can spend as much time with you as you'd like, so maybe we should be friends.' Then he played this old Bob Dylan song I used to hear at his father's house. You know, the one that goes, 'No, no, no, it ain't me, babe,/it ain't me you're looking for, babe'?"

"Ugh," Lina said.

"Like father, like son," Mads said.

"It was a total shock." Holly's tough-guy act was breaking down. She was getting teary again. She didn't have the strength to stop it. "I never saw it coming. I thought everything was fine. I thought we were in love!"

She started full-on crying. It was the surprise that bothered her the most. She'd thought she had everything under control. Then Rob pulled the rug out from under her. That scared her. If it could happen once, it could happen again. And again and again. How could she protect herself?

Mads and Lina hugged her. Mads passed her a handful of Kleenex. "You'll be okay," Lina said.

"You're better off without him," Mads said.

"You're too good for him," Lina said. "You can do way better."

"I know that," Holly said. "But it still hurts."

"We should write a quiz about this," Mads said. "You know, like, 'What are the signs you're about to get dumped?'"

"Mads," Lina said.

"No, she's right," Holly said. "It happens all the time. We should warn others."

Holly, Lina, and Mads' school blog, the Dating Game, featured love quizzes, matchmaking question-naires, advice columns, and anything else they felt like putting on it. By now it was practically an institution at their school, the Rosewood School for Alternative Gifted Education, otherwise known as RSAGE.

"You know what you need?" Mads said. "New blood. Nothing helps you forget a guy like another guy."

"I don't know," Holly said. "I'm kind of sick of guys."

"You're just sick of *Rob*," Mads said. "He represents all guys to you. But he's just a lower form of guy. There are higher forms to be found."

"Please," Holly said. "What percentage of the total male population could be a higher life-form? It must be tiny, like two percent."

"Maybe five percent," Lina said.

"All right, if you want to be optimistic," Holly said. "Five percent. So out of all the guys at RSAGE, there are maybe—*maybe*—twenty good ones. And at least two of them are taken—by you." Lina and Mads were both enjoying happy times with their new boyfriends, Walker Moore and Stephen Costello. "What are the chances that I'm going to bond with one of the few higher life-forms left?"

"You could date outside of school," Mads said. "That gives you much better chances."

"But how will I meet a guy who doesn't go to our school?" Holly asked. "And even if I meet someone, it takes time to figure out if I like him and he likes me and if he's a decent person or if he's got bodies buried in his backyard. . . ." She dropped her head on the kitchen counter and moaned. "I'm doomed. I'll never have another boyfriend as long as I live! The odds are just too low!"

"That's ridiculous," Lina said. "It feels that way now, but you'll find a new guy before you know it."

"What if we speed things up?" Mads said. "Like, what if you could meet twenty guys at once? Wouldn't it be great if you could go to a party and every guy there was available? And you could spend the whole party flirting and talking and by the time it was over, all you had to do was choose one?"

"Sure it would," Holly said. "I'd also like to be Prince William's girlfriend, but it's not going to happen."

"Don't say that!" Mads cried. "I need my illusions. I'm still clinging to that one."

"Mads is onto something," Lina said. "We could hold our own party, singles only. They can casually see how they like each other without having to go on a million blind dates. And they won't have to worry that they're wasting time flirting with people who are already taken."

"Speed Dating!" Mads said. "We'll give you a certain amount of time—five or six minutes—to talk to each guy, and by the end of the party you'll get matched with the one you like best."

"Who also likes you," Lina said.

"No muss, no fuss," Mads said.

"I guess it could be fun," Holly said.

"We'll open it up to kids from other schools," Mads said. "You're bound to meet a new guy that way."

"And if you don't, we'll just keep having parties until you find The One," Lina said. "It's perfect for busy students. It will only take an hour or two a week."

"Let's do it." Holly straightened up, some of her old moxie returning. The memory of Rob's teddy-bear head, which had been making her cry all morning, was fading already. "Even if I don't meet a guy right away, it would be fun to make some friends at other schools. The RSAGE social scene could use some new life. New parties! New people! All right!"

"Yay!" Mads clapped. "Speed Dating!"

"I was getting kind of sick of Rob anyway," Holly said. "I just didn't realize it."

"You're a quick healer. I guess we won't be needing this anymore." Lina started putting the ice cream in the freezer.

"Hey, where are you going with that?" Holly said. "I may be on the mend, but the doctor says I need to keep taking my medicine until I'm one hundred percent cured. Right, Doctor?" She looked at Mads, the Bringer of Ice Cream.

"Absolutely," Mads said. "Keep that Chocolate Brainwash coming."

QUIZ: IS HE GOING TO BREAK UP WITH YOU?
Is the end near? Do you know the signs?
Take this quiz and see which direction your relationship is headed.

1. When you call him, you get his voicemail more than half the time.
   ☐ True: Go to #2.   ☐ False: Go to #3.

2. **He has recently stood you up without a good explanation.**
    ☐ True: Go to #4.   ☐ False: Go to #5.

3. **His pet name for you is something sweet, like Sugar or Honey.**
    ☐ True: Go to #6.   ☐ False: Go to #5.

4. **He named his dog after you.**
    ☐ True: Go to #7.   ☐ False: Go to #8.

5. **He keeps saying you're too good for him.**
    ☐ True: Go to #7.   ☐ False: Go to #9.

6. **He calls you several times a day just to say hi.**
    ☐ True: Go to #9.   ☐ False: Go to #8.

7. **He never calls unless you call him first.**
    ☐ True: Go to Yes.   ☐ False: Go to Maybe.

8. **He remembers your birthday without a reminder.**
    ☐ True: Go to No.   ☐ False: Go to #7.

9. **When he picks you up for a date, he enjoys bantering with your parents.**
    ☐ True: Go to No.   ☐ False: Go to Maybe.

Scoring:

NO: No, he's probably not planning on breaking up with you. Your relationship is on solid ground. You've got yourself a sweetie!

MAYBE: There are a few signs of trouble, but it won't necessarily lead to a breakup if you address them before things careen out of control.

YES: Yes, I'm afraid it doesn't look good for you and your honey. He shows all the classic signs of squirming, restlessness, and attempting to weasel out. You might want to consider a preemptive strike to cut your losses and salvage your dignity. Try Speed Dating (see below), and better luck next time.

"The funny thing is, Rob didn't send me any of these signals," Holly said. "And he still broke up with me."

"Maybe he's extra sneaky," Mads said.

"No system is foolproof," Lina said.

Looking for love? In a hurry? Who isn't? Try Speed Dating! Meet fifteen guys or girls in one afternoon. Talk to each one for six minutes, decide if you like him or her, and we'll take it from there. High school students from all over the Carlton Bay area are eligible. First Speed Dating party: This Saturday, 3 to 5 P.M., in the back garden at Vineland Café. Sign up today! Space is limited, so hurry!

2 Current Mood: Swingy

HERE IS TODAY'S HOROSCOPE: CANCER: There's a difference between expressing yourself and airing your dirty laundry . . . as you are about to find out.

Mood Swing
By Lina Ozu
Current Mood: Perplexed

Spring is here! Bringing the pitter-patter of gossiping tongues. Why so much griping, girls? You say the boys are lazy? They're not asking anyone out? There's even been a rash of breakups! What's the matter with you, boys? Don't you know that this is the best time of year for roaming through flea markets, afternoon strolls, and kisses under the dogwood trees? (Typical boy: "Duh, what?" Just step around that puddle of drool at his feet.)

Well, girls and boys, it doesn't have to be that way. At least one RSAGE dude—let's call him Peter—knows how to celebrate spring right. After overcoming many obstacles—such as other girlfriends, hopeless crushes, and silly arguments— Peter and his new girlfriend, Tess, have finally settled into a groove. I was sitting at Vineland the other day when Tess told me all about it.

Last weekend Peter's mother had a date, so to help her out, Pete and Tess took Pete's little brothers to the county fair. They marched right past all the farmhouse cheeses and artisanal lemonade to the honky-tonk—the games, the rides, the junk food. Which is, as everyone knows, the best part of any fair.

They rode the roller coaster with Pete's brothers, and played Squirt the Clown and Shoot the Ducks. Pete's a good shot: He won each boy a cap gun, and a pink elephant for Tess. They ate hot dogs and ice cream. Pete and Tess rode through the haunted house together and Pete held her hand, even though it wasn't the least bit scary. Even the boys said it was lame. Then they said they wanted to go again. It was a balmy, starry spring night. Tess hadn't felt so happy in a long time.

Pete and Tess rode the Ferris wheel together. Their ride was almost over. It had stopped to let passengers off, and Pete and

Tess's car was stalled at the top. They could see the whole town laid out before them. Pete touched Tess's neck and felt something sticky and pink. Somehow she'd gotten cotton candy on her neck. "Hold still," he said. And he licked the cotton candy off her neck. He licked her neck clean. When there was no more cotton candy left, they kissed until the carny who ran the ride had to tap them on the shoulder and tell them to get the heck off. (Yes, he actually said "heck." Guess it's a carny thing.)

I'm telling this story to help out my sisters in misery. Boys, let Pete be an example for you. He's sweet, he's romantic, he can lick a girl's neck clean. Don't you feel a sudden urge to find a nice girl and hold her hand under the stars? Don't be shy. Do it! NOW!

"Do you like my new column?" Lina asked Walker. She'd posted Mood Swing on the Dating Game mostly because she was in the mood to celebrate her newfound happiness with Walker.

"I guess it's okay," Walker said. "As long as nobody figures out it's really you and me. I mean, when I licked that cotton candy off your neck, I didn't expect the whole school to find out."

He and Lina were sharing a bag of Raisinets in the office of *The Seer*, the school newspaper. They were both sports reporters, finishing up their stories before classes began for the day. Walker dipped his long brown fingers into the bag, tossed a Raisinet into the air, and caught it in his mouth. He was lanky and handsome, his black hair poking off his head in short, stiff spikes.

Lina, medium-tall, slim, and athletic, had straight, shiny black hair and a pretty oval face. "How could anyone figure it out?" she said. "I changed our names. Maybe I should have said you have sisters instead of brothers, to throw people off a little. But, still—I don't think anyone will guess."

"It's just a little embarrassing," Walker said. "All that neck-licking and all. It's personal."

"I don't mean to make it so personal," Lina said. "I'm just trying to write about the state of mind of everyone at school. You know, the zeitgeist. I'm thinking of submitting these columns for the *Crier*'s summer internship." The *Carlton Bay Crier* was a local newspaper. "They only take one high school student a year, so it's pretty competitive. But I think I can show how well I can write and cover student concerns if I publish a regular column on the Dating Game."

"Why don't you just use your clips from the school paper?" Walker asked.

"Sports? Badminton Smackdown? I don't know. Somehow it doesn't seem substantial enough."

"And describing our dates is?"

"That's not *all* I'm going to write about," Lina said.

"You'll see. Anyway, Autumn is applying for the internship too, and she's using *her* blog for clips." Autumn Nelson was a fellow tenth grader whose blog, Nuclear Autumn, was a school must-read. "I'm afraid my sports stories will seem bland next to her, um, colorful self-expression."

"You mean, totally self-indulgent whining sprinkled with mean-spirited gossip?" Walker said. "Come on, Lina."

"Well," Lina said, "the *Crier* only has one spot for a high school student, and writers from other schools are applying, too. It's a tough world out there. I'm going to do whatever it takes."

"Okay," Walker said. "As long as I can pretend I don't know anything about it."

"Be my guest," Lina said.

"So who are Tess and Peter?" Autumn asked. She and her friend Rebecca Hulse uncharacteristically descended upon Lina, Holly, and Mads at lunchtime that afternoon. To Lina's surprise, Mood Swing was the buzz of the school. "Anyone we know? Obviously we must know them, if you know them and they go to this school."

"What difference does it make?" Lina said. "The important thing is the point I was trying to get across, the message I was trying to send to the boys—"

"I've got to find out who Peter is," Rebecca said. "I

want a boy who licks cotton candy off my neck. Whoever that Tess is, she'd better look out. I'm going to swipe that boy of hers away."

Lina blanched, then recovered. Her identity was still safe. For now. Mads and Holly were in on the secret, but besides Walker, that was it. "You know, I might have exaggerated that whole thing, just a little. And how do you know Tess wasn't exaggerating when she told me? Maybe the truth was he saw a little sticky stuff on her neck and wiped it off. End of story. No need for people to go around swiping other people's boyfriends." Rebecca— slim, blond, and glamorous—made Lina nervous. No one would want Rebecca to zero in on her boyfriend. She'd be a formidable rival.

"Well, you said it yourself," Rebecca said. "This place is a desert." She was on the outs with her boyfriend, David Kim. "No water for miles around, and I'm thirsty!"

"I know how to fix that," Mads said. "Come to the Speed Dating party."

"Oh, yeah, I saw that on your blog," Autumn said. "Do you really think you can learn enough about a guy in six minutes to decide if you want to go out with him or not?"

"We'll find out," Holly said. "It's an experiment. And I don't mind being a guinea pig."

"Everybody knows *you're* up for anything, Holly,"

Rebecca said. "The question is, is it worth *our* time? We'd better get back to our table before we lose our prime real estate. Come on, Autumn."

They returned to their usual centrally located table to schmooze with their friends Claire Kessler and Ingrid Bauman.

"Hello, Holly and Mads. Hello, *Tess*." Ramona Fernandez cast a shadow over the table in her corseted black dress, purple tights, black boots, and heavy Goth makeup. It occurred to Lina that Ramona and her shadow were not easy to tell apart.

"My name is not Tess," Lina said to Ramona. "As you know perfectly well. Unless you've experienced some recent head trauma. Which, knowing your headbanger taste in music, is not that unlikely."

"Deathzilla is not a headbanger band," Ramona said. "Donald Death writes sensitive songs about the futility of life in this cold, cruel world. It just happens that you can't sing about that subject without screaming a lot. Not believably, anyway." Deathzilla was Ramona's latest Goth band obsession, and Donald Death was its white-faced, pointy-black-eyebrowed lead singer. "But we're getting off the subject." Ramona dropped her tray and sat down without waiting to be invited. "I didn't know you liked cotton candy so much. What do you do, bathe in it? Or just dab it on your pulse points, like perfume?"

Lina glanced at Mads and Holly, who pretended to be fascinated by something on the wall across the room. Lina and Ramona were friendly, in an itchy, combative way. But Ramona wasn't part of their circle of three. "What are you talking about?"

"Don't be coy," Ramona said. "It's obvious that Tess and Peter are you and Walker. Walker's mother is a widow, right? So she probably dates. And he has two younger brothers. And going to the county fair is just the kind of cornball activity you'd think is cute. But here's the clincher: You've got a big pink stuffed elephant in your locker. How stupid do you think people are? If they don't know it now, it won't be long."

Lina didn't think anyone had seen the elephant. She waved this away. "I am not the kind of person who thinks going to the county fair is cute. Generally. I made an exception in this case. But anyway, nobody knows that about me. You don't even know it about me. You're just guessing."

"I still say you'll be unmasked before you know it," Ramona said. "And what will Walker think of that? He comes off so whipped in your column. It could be pretty embarrassing for him."

Lina remembered what Walker had said earlier. The last thing she wanted to do was embarrass him, or herself.

But she still felt confident that their identities were safe.

"You're just trying to upset me," Lina said to Ramona. "You're not applying for the *Crier's* summer internship program, by any chance, are you?" Maybe Ramona was trying to psych her out.

Ramona grinned. "Of course, I am. After all, I'm the editor of the school literary magazine—and I'm only a sophomore. Erica Howard already told me she found that impressive."

"Who's Erica Howard?" Mads asked.

"The Metro editor at the *Crier*," Lina said. "She's in charge of the interns. They take a few college students and one 'unusually precocious high school student.'"

"That wording is key," Ramona said. "'*Unusually* precocious.' Not just ordinary, everyday smart. Like most people. When it comes to unusual, I've got you and Autumn beat by a mile."

"She said 'unusual,' not 'freakish,'" Lina said.

"There's no point in arguing about it," Ramona said. "The final results will vindicate me. I'm submitting some of my latest poems. If Erica Howard has any brains, she'll recognize genius when she sees it."

"I'm sure she'll love your latest sonnet, 'A Worm's Thoughts at Mealtime,'" Lina said. "In case you didn't read the latest issue of *Inchworm*," she explained to Holly and

Mads, "it tells what a worm is thinking while it gnaws on Ramona's grandmother's corpse."

"Ew," Mads and Holly said together.

"The journal is called *Inchworm*, and nobody ever writes about worms," Ramona said. "The worm takes everyone after they die. No one is exempt. Except people who get cremated. I think. Do worms eat ashes?"

"You think I know?" Holly said.

"You have to admit it's unusually precocious," Ramona said.

"Or just creepy," Lina said.

"It's better than a sappy story about the county fair," Ramona said.

"At least that's of local interest," Lina said.

"You are going to get busted for that story," Ramona said. "Everyone will figure out who Pete and Tess are, eventually. And then you'll know what it feels like to weather a storm of ridicule."

"Like you do every day?" Lina said.

"Precisely."

Ramona had a knack for finding Lina's sensitive spots—and a tendency to be negative. *It's nothing to worry about,* Lina told herself. *Just Ramona being Ramona. That is, a pain.*

3 The New Girl's Got It Going On

HERE IS TODAY'S HOROSCOPE: VIRGO: You will encounter a sticky romantic problem, and you won't be able to un-stick it until you get that glue off your fingers.

Y ou look so cute on roller skates," Stephen said. Mads snuggled against him in the compact backseat of his red Mini-Cooper. She wore jeans and a red cowgirl shirt that had actually come from a kids' store. She was petite, still small enough to wear children's sizes, though she preferred not to, unless it was something kitschy-cool, like the cowgirl shirt. She wore a red bandanna in her dark hair and looked up at Stephen with her small, sleepy eyes.

"Who doesn't look good on skates?" Mads said. "Especially under a disco ball, with Jed Cheatham on the Mighty Wurlitzer. It's the equivalent of a camera lens smeared with Vaseline—makes everybody look great."

They'd gone to an old roller rink Stephen had found way out of town, where instead of dance music an old man played a Wurlitzer organ while couples waltzed on roller skates. The men wore 1950s Elvis clothes, and the women wore full skirts that swirled around their legs. Mads and Stephen felt awkward in their jeans and lack of waltzing ability, but still, it was fun. The old four-wheeled roller skates they rented were clunky compared with the Rollerblades they were used to. Stephen, tall and skinny and serious-faced, grinned goofily when he tried to waltz.

"I love the way you're always slightly off-balance," Stephen said. "Just when I think you're about to fall down, you wave your arms or grab the rail and save yourself. It's the suspense. Like a horror movie. Will she fall? Oh, no! . . . she's okay . . . no, wait . . . there she goes! . . . caught herself again—"

"Yeah? Well, there's no suspense watching you," Mads said. "You fall on your butt every five minutes. I could set my watch to it. And yet, no matter how many times I see it, it's still funny."

"Funny-strange or funny-ha-ha?" Stephen asked.

"Funny-sexy," Mads said.

"Funny-sexy?" Stephen repeated. "What does that mean? It doesn't really make sense—"

"Quiet, you." She stared at him in the dark for a second. The streetlight made his eyes glow. "I don't have to make sense. I'm Madison, Queen of the Wild Frontier." She closed her eyes, and he kissed her.

They hadn't been going out for very long, and Stephen had been away in Europe with his mother for several weeks, so they were still shy and tentative with each other. Stephen pressed his lips against hers, and her head tilted back awkwardly. She didn't try to move or say anything. She didn't want to spoil the moment.

But she felt stiff, and her mind wandered. She remembered something she'd read in *Cosmo* that month, an article about kissing tips. Something about a counterclockwise tongue-swirl that could drive a boy wild. She decided to try it. Maybe that would warm things up between them. She wanted to show Stephen he didn't have to be shy with her. That she could be as wild as any cowgirl.

She gathered up her courage and went for it. She opened her lips and pushed her tongue out, pressing against Stephen's teeth. For a second, he relaxed. His mouth opened, and he let her tongue roam around in there. Then he suddenly snapped his mouth shut, nearly biting her tongue off, and jolted up as if he'd been electrocuted.

"What's the matter?" Mads asked.

"What? Oh, nothing," Stephen said.

Nothing? It sure didn't seem like nothing to her.

"Something just poked me in the butt," Stephen said. "I think there's a loose spring in the car seat or something."

"Oh." Mads wanted to buy it, she really did. But come on. A loose spring? In a year-old car?

"What did it feel like?" Mads asked. "Did it feel like this?" She playfully pinched his butt. He twitched and laughed.

"No, it was more like *this*." He tried to pinch her, but she dodged him. They played around like this in the backseat, pinching each other and slapping each other's hands away and laughing. But the sexy mood was gone, and they never got around to serious kissing again that night. The porch light on Mads' house started blinking, her mother's sign that she knew Mads was home and it was time to come in or face the consequences, which involved her mother coming out there herself and knocking on the car window. Obviously, Mads would eat live spiders to avoid that.

"There's the signal," Mads said, pushing the front seat up and opening the car door.

Stephen clambered out after her and kissed her quickly before she trotted up the stone steps to her house. "Happy trails."

When the new girl, Quintana Rhea, walked into school on Monday morning, Mads felt it right away. Something different. Electricity.

Quintana had long, glossy, straight brown hair that moved like water across her shoulders. She was small-chested, with a cute little bubble butt. Her lips were very red, and her teeth very white. Her hazel eyes were large and fringed with thick, black lashes. And she was wearing a chic pink-and-silver-sequined-covered peasant blouse that Mads had seen in *Teen Vogue* only a week before. Quintana was very pretty and very chic. But that wasn't it.

Mads wasn't the only one who noticed her. Heads turned as she passed through the halls. Boys, with a helpless look in their eyes, watched her walk until she turned the corner. Girls, too, with a different sort of helplessness. She had something that couldn't be bought. But, what? Mads turned the question over in her mind. What, exactly, was it?

By lunch on day one, Quintana trailed a stream of boys in her wake wherever she went. All kinds of boys: lowly freshmen, hottie seniors, regular in-between guys.

They didn't seem to care that they were part of an endless stream. They just wanted to be near her. They wafted after her like perfume.

What's her secret? Mads wondered as she watched Quintana scan the lunchroom for a place to sit. Because Mads knew she had one. It leaked out of her pores, whatever it was. Quintana seemed to know something. Something juicy.

"Is that the new girl?" Holly asked.

"Yeah," Mads said. "She was in my English class. Her name's Quintana. She moved here from L.A."

"I feel sorry for her, starting so late in the school year," Lina said.

Quintana spotted Autumn, Rebecca, and Ingrid at their table and headed toward them.

"This should be interesting," Holly said.

Quintana stood in front of Rebecca and her friends. She nodded at an empty seat, and Mads could tell she was asking if it was taken. Rebecca looked at the other girls. Then she did that thing where she showed her teeth as if she were smiling, but somehow it didn't come off as friendly. She said something to Quintana, who didn't seem to react. She just shrugged and walked away, as if saying, "Your loss."

"Those bitches," Holly said.

"She doesn't look too upset about it, though," Lina said.

"I'll go get her," Mads said. She imagined Quintana scurrying for the door, ready to dump her uneaten lunch in the trash and spend the rest of the period in the bathroom, crying. At least that's what Mads would have done. But Quintana just looked around for another table with another empty spot. Mads walked up to her.

"Hey." Mads tapped her on the shoulder. "We've got room at our table. Want to sit with us?"

Quintana smiled, as if she'd been expecting this all along. "Thanks," she said. She followed Mads back to the table. Mads introduced Lina and Holly.

"Rebecca can be cold," Holly said. "But she's not as scary as she tries to make herself look."

"Yeah, she's like a blowfish," Lina said. "She puffs herself up to intimidate you, but she's as insecure as anybody else. If not more. She just doesn't want you to know it."

"That blowfish technique works pretty well," Quintana said. "But I'm used to it. I've moved so many times, I'm an expert at being the new girl. This is my third school this year."

"Wow," Lina said. "That's rough."

"It's not so bad," Quintana said. "I like living in different places. Before L.A. we lived in Honolulu, and before that, Dallas. My dad's a business consultant. He works for a new company every six months or so."

"I still think it would be hard to change schools all the time," Mads said.

"You learn to be tough," Quintana said. "Every school has its little quirks you have to adjust to. I've adopted so many quirks, I'm getting to be kind of quirky myself." She laughed, low and throaty. An oddly adult laugh for a tenth grader.

"People are pretty friendly here, once you get to know them," Mads said.

"We're a little lacking in cute boyage, that's our biggest problem," Holly said.

"Oh, I don't know," Quintana said. "I met some pretty cute guys this morning. Let's see, there was Mo, and Alex, and David, and this extreme hottie who offered to share his muffin with me . . . Sean? I think it was Sean."

"You met all those guys in your first three hours?" Lina asked.

"You met Sean?" Mads was impressed—and a little jealous. Sean Benedetto was a senior and the school's major hottie. As a ninth grader, Mads had taken one look at him and vowed that someday he would be hers. Now, a year and a half later, she still had a long way to go. But the goal was always there in the back of her mind. Sean. He was her ideal guy. It took her a year and a half to get him to notice she was alive. And he was offering Quintana a muffin on her first day? Why was life so unfair?

"Why, is he a big deal?" Quintana took the top off her hamburger bun, smothered the meat patty in ketchup, then cut into it with her knife and fork.

"Kind of," Mads said.

"To Mads, he is," Lina said.

"Not just to me," Mads said. "He's the sex god of Rosewood."

"Granted," Holly said. "But that's only because there's so little competition."

Quintana laughed that low laugh again. "Madison, you can't let boys intimidate you. If you give them too much power, they get so out of hand."

She finished three-quarters of her hamburger, wiped her mouth with her napkin, and took a tube of lip gloss from her bag. She swiped it across her lips. It was a bright magenta color with gold sparkles in it.

"I love your lip gloss," Mads said. "What kind is it?"

"Munchies," Quintana said. "Try some." She handed the tube to Mads. "I don't wear it for the color so much as the flavors."

Mads dabbed the gloss on and licked her lips. "It tastes like . . . what is that? Chili pepper?"

"Jalapeño," Quintana said. "It comes in regular flavors like mint and cinnamon, but you can also get chocolate, vanilla, pepperoni pizza, and taco. Boys love it. If you wear this while a boy is kissing you, he'll go crazy. They can't get enough of it. It's like they want to eat your lips."

"Wow," Mads said, memorizing the label on the tube. "I've got to get some." Maybe this lip gloss was just what she needed to spice things up with Stephen.

Her instinct about Quintana was turning out to be right: She knew a lot of things. Useful things. Boy things. Already she'd given Mads info she could really use. Maybe Rebecca and Autumn didn't want to be friends with her, but Mads thought they were foolish. Quintana knew boys, and Mads wasn't going to pass up a chance to learn everything she could.

4 At the Tone, the Time Will Be . . .

To:	hollygolitely
From:	your daily horoscope

HERE IS TODAY'S HOROSCOPE: CAPRICORN: A mysterious stranger will enter your life today, so make sure you're wearing clean underwear.

olly glanced around the ivy-covered garden at Vineland Café, a favorite coffee hangout for RSAGE students, checking out the fifteen guys who huddled near the chips and salsa. The first Speed Dating party was being held that afternoon. Kids from schools all over the Carlton Bay area had clamored for a spot, but Holly thought they should limit enrollment or the whole process could take hours. So they signed up the first fifteen girls and fifteen guys. Holly was number one on the list.

"This should be good," Sebastiano Altman-Peck whispered to Holly. Her locker neighbor at school, he was slinky and snake-hipped, with abundant loose brown curls any girl would envy, an elegant Roman nose, and full lips. Basically Michelangelo's David without the muscles and with a smart mouth.

"You didn't sign up, did you?" Holly asked. "I don't remember seeing your name."

"Me? No. I'd never put myself through a meat-grinder like this. I'm just here to witness the carnage."

"Well, go sit down someplace." Holly shooed him toward a white iron table, away from the Speed Dating party. "You're making me nervous."

Sebastiano ignored her. "There's that new girl." He was looking at Quintana. "She's hot."

"Mads says that, too," Holly said. "What's so hot about her? She's pretty, but there are lots of girls at school just as pretty as she is."

"There's just something about her," Sebastiano said. "She looks so, I don't know . . . at home in her skin. Like a cat. Or a wild animal."

"'A wild animal,'" Holly scoffed. "That's just a stupid boy fantasy. Wild animals don't wear padded bras."

"In this nature preserve, they do." He caught Holly's irritated glance and added, "She can't hold a candle to you, of course, Boobmeister." Holly winced slightly at Sebastiano's favorite nickname for her, which Mads had started as a good-natured joke about Holly's bustiness. "I don't see anyone here good enough for you," he said, scanning the crowd. "You deserve someone out of the ordinary. These guys, I don't know . . ."

"Don't doom me before the party even starts," Holly said. "I've got to give them a chance."

"Be my guest. But I'm not seeing you with *that*." He nodded at a squat guy wearing an extra-large T-shirt over extra-large shorts barely clinging to his butt.

"It's just like you to pick out the worst offender," Holly said. "That's one guy out of fifteen."

Sebastiano nodded toward another boy, who was stuffing his face with chips.

"All right, two out of fifteen," Holly said. "That still leaves thirteen chances to find love. And if it doesn't work out today, we'll just hold another Speed Dating party. There are plenty more kids who want to try it."

Mads clapped her hands. "Okay, ready to start? Girls, sit down where you see your name." She'd set up a long table with fifteen chairs on each side. The girls would stay seated while the boys moved from one girl to the next every six minutes. After each meeting, the boys and girls would jot down notes about each other, and then meet the next candidate. At the end, everyone would hand in their scorecards and Mads, Holly, and Lina would compare the notes and make matches based on the comments.

Holly took her place in the middle of the table. To her left sat Ramona Fernandez and two of her Goth friends, Siobhan Gallagher and Chandra Bledsoe.

"Ramona?" Holly said. "I'm surprised to see you here."

"Are you kidding?" Ramona said. "Pass up a chance to ridicule fifteen guys to their face—*and* behind their backs? We wouldn't miss it."

Great. Already, people weren't taking this seriously. Holly hoped at least some of the boys were actually looking to go out with a girl, and not just joke around.

Lina sat at a table behind a big alarm clock. "Okay," she said. "Remember, you have six minutes to talk to each person, then it's time to switch. Are you ready? Boys take your places."

The boys, wearing name tags, lined up and sat down across from the girls. Three boys scuffled over to the seat across from Quintana.

"You'll get a chance to talk to everyone," Mads said. "Just sit anywhere."

Finally everyone settled down at the long table.

Holly looked at the boy in front of her. He had a round face and very short hair. He smiled at her. He had something green stuck in his teeth.

"Ready?" Mads shouted. "Go!"

"Hi, Holly, it's nice to meet you," the boy said. "I'm talking really fast so you can know all about me in six minutes. Where should I start? There's so much to say. Um, I play baseball, but I'm not shooting for pro or anything, I just like to play. . . ."

Holly stared at his name tag so she would have something to look at besides the spinach in his teeth. Jon Pinchbeck. Jon Pinchbeck. Jon Pinchbeck. Okay, this was getting boring. She looked up. No! Spinach! She looked down again. Red T-shirt. Red T-shirt. Nice shade of tomato red. Spinach and tomato go well together. . . .

"So, what about you?" Jon asked her. "What's your favorite subject in school? Do you have any hobbies?"

"I like geometry," Holly said. "And Spanish and biology. And my hobbies are, um, let's see, I enjoy brushing my teeth, and flossing can be fun—"

That got a blank stare. Holly glanced at the clock on the table. Four minutes to go! Who knew six minutes could feel so endless?

She struggled to come up with something interesting to say about herself. "I play tennis, and I love to swim in the summer. . . ." Why did she suddenly feel so boring? She didn't usually think of herself that way. Her friends never called her dull. But she wished she'd gone to camp in Peru, or volunteered to save the endangered purple stinkbeetle—anything to have something to talk about besides school.

Next to her she could hear Ramona saying, "I am a Mistress of the Night. I know how to make love potions and voodoo dolls. It doesn't matter if you like me or not, because if I like you, I can *make* you like me. And if I *don't* like you—you'd better run." Holly couldn't resist a glance at the face of the boy Ramona was speaking to. Just as she'd suspected: frozen with terror. At least Ramona wasn't boring.

"—but, you know, I do like to watch baseball with my dad once in a while," Holly heard herself saying. Jon Pinchbeck's eyes glazed over. At least he'd closed his mouth, so she didn't have to see the spinach in his teeth anymore. The alarm clock buzzed. "Time's up!" Lina shouted. Thank god.

"Nice meeting you," Jon Pinchbeck said as he got up to move across from Ramona. Holly silently wished him luck. Then she picked up her pen and marked her scorecard next to Boy #1: Oral hygiene. Enough said.

Boy #2 sat down and grinned at her. Perfect, spinach-free teeth. What a relief.

Gus Anastas. He wasn't bad-looking: olive skin, even features, black hair in a short, modified pompadour. A jutting chin. The fuzzy upper lip would have to go, but that was easily taken care of. His aura was a little bland, but that was a common boy pitfall. Sometimes, once you got to know them . . .

"Okay, first, I've just got to say that you are, like, really hot, okay? I mean, whoa, Mama! Mm-mm—mm. I noticed you as soon as I got here. I looked around to pick out the filthiest girl in the place 'cause I knew I wasn't going to waste a lot of time talking to a dog, you know what I'm sayin'? Even six minutes is too long. And you are smokin'. Like Kansas City barbecue. Oh yeah. And finger-lickin' good, too, I bet. Am I right? Am I right?"

Holly stared at him. She knew her mouth was hanging open, yet somehow she couldn't find the strength to close it. How did this person exist in civilization as she knew it?

"Quiet type, huh? I like that. I can't stand those bitches who just yap, yap, yap—"

"You might as well move along now," Holly said quietly. "Because the day I go out with you is the day I lose all hope for mankind, and frankly, on that day I'd rather suffer alone."

"Tough girl, huh?" Gus said. "That's okay, I like 'em

when they play hard to get. The chase is half the fun, right? But we both know what happens at the end." He leaned forward and suggestively wiggled his eyebrows at her. Some kind of acid liquid burbled up from her stomach into the back of her throat. She swallowed it down, hoping she wasn't about to throw up.

"Please—just get away from me," she said.

The alarm clock mercifully buzzed, and she gladly fed Gus Anastas to the gaping jaws of Ramona. She marked her score card. Boy #2: Asshole.

Boy #3 was a familiar face: Jay Mukherjee, from her parents' country club. Holly's parents played golf and tennis with Jay's from time to time.

"Hey, Holly," he said. "Haven't seen you since the Christmas dance at the club. You're looking good."

"Thanks, so are you." She'd known him since sixth grade—not well, but well enough. If sparks were going to fly between them, wouldn't it have happened by now? Maybe not. Maybe he'd changed. Maybe he'd cultivated some exciting new personality trait she'd never seen before. Like race car driving, or bank robbery . . .

"So, you teaching tennis at the club this summer?" he asked.

"I don't know yet," she said. "You?"

"Probably. Same every year. It's fun, though. I like

hanging with the kids. Did you know Martin Crisp is going to Yale next year?"

"Really?" She tried to remember which of the hordes of bland, nice-enough guys at the club was Martin Crisp. Oh, yeah. The one who always replaced the alligator on his polo shirt with a tiny bulldog. Cute. He'd known he was going to Yale since before he could pronounce it.

"But guess what—Kent Schweitzer didn't get into Harvard. Can you believe that? And he's a double legacy!"

"Really?" *Who cares?* Holly thought.

"So he's going to Amherst," Jay said. "That's still a good school."

"Uh-huh."

"My mother's on the planning committee for the Picnic this year," Jay said. The Picnic was the first big social event of the Carlton Bay Country Club's summer calendar. It involved a lot of halfhearted family games, super-competitive swim meets and tennis matches, and lemonade spiked with vodka. Holly had been hoping to get out of it this year.

"Are you going?" Jay asked her. "Maybe we could go together. I've got two tennis matches that day, but we could be partners in the three-legged race."

"Um—"

Buzz! "Time!" Lina called. *Aw, too bad.*

"I'll let you know," Holly said as Jay stood up. "I think we'll be away that weekend."

Boy #3: Boring, she wrote. And too much in common with her family. She needed someone fresh. Someone different. Someone surprising. As it was, sitting next to Ramona was more fun than she'd expected. Knowing what each boy would face after her almost made the whole fiasco worthwhile.

Boy #4 was kind of cute, but obsessed with NASCAR. That was *too* different. Boy #5 seemed kind of out of it. (What gave it away? The dilated pupils? Or the fact that he kept calling her "Kelly"?)

Boy #6, she knew from school. Not smart enough. The less said about Boys #7, 8, and 9, the better. She was losing hope. Maybe this Speed Dating thing wasn't such a good idea after all.

Then came Boy #10. He sat down and flashed her a Mona Lisa smile. Coy. Was it a come-on, or was he just very sure of himself? Holly didn't know. All she knew was she couldn't stop looking at him. He was small-boned, maybe a couple inches taller than she was, with a chiseled face, a thatch of straight black hair, and the lithe, muscular figure of a martial arts aficionado. He wore a white button-down shirt. He didn't say hello. He just said, "What time is it?"

"What?" She laughed a little.

He smiled at her. It was a nice smile, and pleasantly lacking in food particles. "Just look at the clock and tell me what time it is."

This was certainly different. "Why? You can see it from where you're sitting," she said. *Unless he has a vision problem,* she thought. *Maybe he's blind and I've just insulted him!* "Can't you?" She waved her hand in front of his face. He wasn't wearing glasses or contacts, as far as she could tell. People who wore contacts usually showed a telltale sign, like eyes too wide open or habitual rabbity blinking.

"I can see it," he said. "But I want you to look at it, too. Just go along with this for a second. It will pay off, I swear."

Holly giggled, mystified but amused. "Okay." Whatever. She looked at the big alarm clock on the table where Mads and Lina were sitting. Mads looked up and waved at her. Holly waved back.

"What time is it?" Boy #10 asked. "Exactly."

"3:17," Holly said.

"3:17," the boy repeated. "That's my new magic number. I'll always remember that I met you at 3:17."

Holly laughed again. "Always? Like, even on your deathbed? Even if we never speak to each other again?"

He nodded. "These are our first six minutes together.

From now on, every Saturday at 3:17, I'll think, *That was my first minute with Holly.* Or maybe second minute, since it took you a minute or so to get around to looking at the clock."

"So should we say 3:16?" Holly asked. "Should 3:16 be the official time of our first meeting?"

"No, let's stick with 3:17," the boy said. "It has a better ring to it."

Holly stared at him, mesmerized. What was he talking about? Whatever it was, she liked it. It wasn't cars, or tennis, or school, or booty. It was just itself.

He had gray eyes, mixed with blue and green and gold. His irises seemed to contain a maze, which she tried to follow with her own eyes. It was too complicated. She got lost.

She waited for him to say something else, but he just gazed back at her as if he could find the meaning of life in her face. The minutes ticked by. At least, Holly assumed they did. She forgot about time. She forgot about everything but that gray maze.

"Time's up!" Lina called.

Boy #10 smiled. The spell was broken.

Holly felt dazed. She watched him stand up, as if she were watching her own dream. He nodded and smiled at her again. Then he sat down in front of Ramona. Holly sensed that a new boy had deposited himself in the seat across from her, but she couldn't bring herself to look at him yet.

Who was that guy? She'd been so caught up in his mesmerizing stare that she'd forgotten to look at his name tag. She leaned toward Ramona to get a glimpse of it. Eli Collins. What a beautiful name.

"Number 11!" Lina shouted. "Go!"

Holly looked up at Boy #11. She could hardly see his face. "Just a sec," she said, and picked up her pen to write something about Eli Collins. "Boy #10," she wrote. "3:17."

Boy #11 started talking, but she barely heard him. She hardly looked at or listened to another boy for the rest of the party. Her eyes kept straying toward Eli. Was what he had said to her just a schtick, a line? Was he pulling the same trick on other girls?

He chatted easily with Ramona, and Holly didn't once see her glance at the clock. Ramona looked uncharacteristically charmed by him, but she wasn't his type.

As the boys streamed past her, Holly watched him with the next girl and the next. She saw him talking and laughing and listening. But never once did he sit and stare at the girl as he had with her.

So it wasn't an act. Maybe.

"Yoo hoo, Holly. Over here." Boy #15 waved his

hand in front of her eyes, trying to get her attention. "I always have the same problem," the boy said. "Girls never listen to me. It's like I'm invisible! Or inaudible?"

"You're perfectly audible," she told him, just to be nice, because she didn't hear another word he said. Maybe it wasn't fair, but that was the way things were. Her decision was made. There was one boy for her, and one boy only.

Eli Collins.

5 Busted

HERE IS TODAY'S HOROSCOPE: CANCER: Everyone's talking about you (behind your back). Just thought you should know.

What about this guy, Holly?" Lina flipped through the Speed Dating Rate Cards, looking for comments on Holly. It was the evening after the first party, and Lina, Holly, and Mads were sitting on Lina's bed with a big bowl of popcorn. "He wrote, 'Whatup, girl? I wanna—' Oh."

"What?" Mads leaned over her shoulder to look.

Lina blushed and turned the card facedown. "It's gross. Let's just say a newspaper wouldn't print it."

"Let me guess: Gus something-or-other, right?" Holly said.

"How did you know?" Mads asked.

"If you'd talked to him, you'd know," Holly said. "I don't care what any of those guys wrote about me. I only want to see one card. Eli Collins. Did you find it yet?"

"Maybe he forgot to turn his card in," Mads said.

"Wait—here it is." Lina peeled apart two rate cards that had been stuck together by a molecule of chewing gum. "Ick. Somebody had gummy fingers. Not Eli, I hope." She looked at the card. It said, "Name: Eli Collins. School: Griffith Academy. E-mail: eli_eli_o." That was all. No comments, no nothing.

"What? What does it say?" Holly snatched the card away from her. She frowned as she read it. "I can't believe he didn't write any comments about me. He stared into my eyes as if he were having a religious experience."

"He didn't rate any other girls, either," Mads said. "Maybe he doesn't like to write. Maybe he's dyslexic or something. Hey, that reminds me of a joke: A dyslexic guy walks into a bra—get it? Walks into a bra?"

But Lina could see that Holly was in no mood for jokes. "That's cute, Mads. Look, Holly, don't worry. If he likes you, he can look you up through school, or through Speed Dating Central. Or in the phone book, even. And

47

if he doesn't, you can always e-mail him yourself."

"Oh, no," Holly said. "I'm not going to e-mail him unless he writes me first. I don't want him to think I like him if he doesn't like me. It's too humiliating."

"Didn't you like *any* of the other guys?" Mads asked. "Most of them sure liked you. What about this one, Jay Mukherjee? He says 'Holly would be perfect for me. I've already gone out with just about every other good-looking girl at our club, so she seems like the next logical choice.'"

"That's inspiring," Holly said.

"Yeah, what a passionate guy," Lina said.

"They were all like that," Holly said. "They all had something wrong with them. All except Eli." She paused, and Lina thought, *This would make a good Mood Swing column—the perils and pitfalls of Speed Dating.*

"I can't stop thinking about him," Holly said.

"But you hardly know him," Mads said. "You hardly even talked to him."

"All he said to you was, 'It's 3:17,'" Lina said.

"It doesn't matter," Holly said. "There's something about him. I'm so curious about him. His mysterious ways got to me. I'm helpless! What if he's my soul mate?"

"Can you find your soul mate in just six minutes?" Lina said.

"Good question," Mads said. "That's basically love at first sight—if you believe in that. Which, of course, I do."

"I'm not sure I do," Lina said. "Do you, Holly?"

"I don't know," Holly said. "I didn't think I did. . . ."

QUIZ: IS HE YOUR SOUL MATE?

You see him, and your heart starts racing. How can you tell if it's the real thing or just your caffeine habit? Take this quiz and see.

1. When you first saw him, you thought:

   a ▶ ew (gag).

   b ▶ eh (shrug).

   c ▶ hmmm . . . (raised eyebrow).

   d ▶ zowie! (steam coming out of ears).

2. How many times have you been in love?

   a ▶ never

   b ▶ once

   c ▶ twice

   d ▶ three to five times

   e ▶ more than five times

3. Why do you love him?

   a ▶ He has curly hair, and you're a sucker for that.

   b ▶ His soul shines through his eyes.

c ▶ Everybody says he's cute.

d ▶ He's so easy to talk to.

4. He's different from other boys because:

a ▶ he really listens.

b ▶ he actually likes musicals.

c ▶ he can dance without looking dorky.

d ▶ he's got a third nipple.

5. You know he loves you because:

a ▶ he said so.

b ▶ he gave you a locket with his picture in it.

c ▶ he gave you half his sandwich.

d ▶ he gave you a hickey.

6. The thing he likes best about you is:

a ▶ your smile lights up the room.

b ▶ he feels comfortable with you.

c ▶ you're pretty.

d ▶ you're always home.

7. You're a perfect match because you share:

a ▶ the same taste in music.

b ▶ unquenchable passion.

c ▶ the same size jeans.

d ▶ the same goals and values.

Scoring:

1. a-0; b-1; c-2; d-3

2. a-4; b-3; c-2; d-1; e-0

3. a-1; b-2; c-0; d-3

4. a-3; b-2; c-1; d-0

5. a-2; b-3; c-1; d-0

6. a-2; b-3; c-1; d-0

7. a-1; b-2; c-0; d-3

0-10: TOTALLY DELUSIONAL

This one is not your soul mate. Why do you keep telling
yourself he is? You probably shouldn't even know this person.
Find someone with more substance. And cut down on your
coffee consumption.

11-17: SOMEWHAT COMPATIBLE

You might be able to make this work, but you will probably
never be soul mates unless one of you matures an awful lot in
the next few weeks.

18-22: SOUL MATES

You're made for each other! Enjoy it. It's a rare thing.

Mood Swing
Current Mood: Sexy

I'm sorry, but Tess's boyfriend Peter has got to be the cutest, sweetest boy on the planet. She told me a little secret about him. The other night they were making out at Tess's house. Her uptight parents were out. Tess doesn't like to have Peter over when they're around, because her mother tends to grill Peter on his academic credentials and his plans for the future. Total buzzkill.

Anyway, back to the good part of the story: Tess found this funny little spot on Peter's stomach, right below his rib cage. They were kissing and everything, getting into it, and she put her hand under his shirt—he has a great long, flat stomach, not really a six-pack, but Tess isn't into muscles anyway—and she's rubbing his stomach and she accidentally presses this spot, right where the ribs make kind of a corner. And he squeaked! This adorable little mousy sound came out of his mouth. So they stopped kissing, and Tess started laughing, and she pressed the same spot again, and he squeaked again! And it turns out all she has to do is press that spot and he squeaks every time! He can't help it. Is that not the sweetest?

So then Tess started saying, "Hey, Mr. Squeaky-Mouse, how would you like a piece of cheese? And she pressed the spot, and Peter squeaked back as if he were a mouse saying, "Yes, please!" They had a whole conversation like this, where Pete was

Squeaky-Mouse. Sometimes Tess pretended to be a cat, and she hissed and scratched at Pete and made him squeak as if he were afraid of her. They laughed so hard, Pete took a sip of Coke and accidentally snorted it up his nose, and it sprayed all over his clothes. He went into the bathroom to clean himself off—and he accidentally left his boxers on the floor, under a towel. Tess didn't know they were there until her mother found them later that evening and waved them in her face with an accusatory scowl. Tess had to think fast. . . .

To be continued . . .

Lina thought of Mood Swing as a kind of secret love letter to Walker, only in public. It gave her a little thrill to think that she was writing her true feelings about him, how adorable she thought he was and how much she liked being with him, and everybody at school could read it, only they didn't know the truth. They didn't know exactly what she was saying or who she was talking about. It was like starring in *Romeo and Juliet*, with your real boyfriend as Romeo.

On top of that, girls kept stopping her in the halls to tell her how much they loved to read about Peter and Tess. "I love to read those really secret details," Claire said. "To find out what people really do when they're making out. It makes me realize I'm not as weird as I thought."

Later that day, Lina stopped by *The Seer's* office to

check her e-mail. She had a message from Erica Howard, the editor in charge of the *Crier* internship. Lina had sent her a link to Mood Swing and asked what she thought of it. Had she read it? Nervously, Lina opened the e-mail.

> To: linaonme
> From: ehoward
> Re: mood swing
> Lina—Thanks for sending me the link to your new column on
> your blog. I'm really enjoying it. You're a natural writer,
> and the antics of Peter and Tess feel very authentic. And
> entertaining. I'm totally addicted. Keep it up. You could
> be the voice of your generation!
> —Erica

All right! Lina thought. *I knew she'd like it! She'll never pick Autumn's blog over mine now.*

Walker came in and sat next to her. She pinched him, gave him a kiss, and said, "Did you read Mood Swing today? Erica Howard just wrote me to say she loves it!"

He looked up at her—he'd been staring at the desktop, tapping a pencil—and scowled. Something was wrong.

"What is it?" Lina asked. "Did something bad happen? I bet if you read my column it would cheer you up."

"I don't think so," Walker said. "Lina, people are onto

us. The Peter and Tess thing, I mean. Rob and I were having an argument in history about the Cuban Missile Crisis, and when I said he was dead wrong, he said, 'Yeah, you're right. I'm a moron. Don't mind me, dude, just step around the puddle of drool.'"

"He did?" Lina vaguely remembered that line about the drool from her first Mood Swing column, when she had accused most of the boys at school—okay, all of them except for "Pete"—of being dumb when it came to girls. "But that doesn't mean anything," she said. "He knows I write the column and that I'm your girlfriend. He's just ribbing you about that. And maybe he's indirectly taking a dig at Holly through me, through you."

"Yeah? That's pretty indirect." Walker stood up and rubbed his spiky hair. "That's not the worst of it. Jake Soros came up to me in the locker room after gym and punched me in the stomach."

Lina gasped. "Did he hurt you? Why did he do that?"

"He said he wanted to find my squeaky spot."

Uh-oh.

Lina tried to lift Walker's shirt to see if he was hurt, but he pulled it down and said, "Stop that. I'm okay."

Mo Basri walked into the office, took one look at Lina and Walker, and said, "Hey Lina. Hey, Squeaky." He tossed a ball of paper in the trash and walked out.

Lina covered her face with her hands. "I don't get it. How do they know? How did they figure it out?"

"I don't know," Walker said. "But I think you'd better stop writing all our secrets in your column. Because I can only take so many punches to the gut."

"But everybody loves it!" Lina said. She could taste the panic rising her throat, bitter and metallic on the back of her tongue. "The Dating Game has gotten more hits than ever since I started Mood Swing. People keep telling me how much they like it. And it could help me win the internship."

Walker grabbed her hand. He was miserable; she could see it in his eyes. And she didn't want to make him miserable.

"Lina, have you read Nuclear Autumn lately?" he asked.

"Nuclear Autumn?" Lina read it occasionally but tried to avoid it, even though it could be juicy. "No. Why?"

Walker pressed some buttons on the keyboard in front of her. "I think you'd better read it."

Nuclear Autumn:
Keeping You Informed of the Latest
Developments in the Life of Autumn Nelson

Okay, hello? Let's stop this "Peter and Tess" charade right now. Lina Ozu, I'm calling you to the mat on this. In case any-

body at RSAGE—which is supposed to be a school for gifted students, if I have to remind you—is too stupid to figure it out on her own, Tess and Peter, who Lina calls her "friends," are really Lina and her boyfriend, Walker Moore, in real life. How stupid do you think we are, Lina? I mean, duh! Anybody could have figured this out, but for those of you who have been on drugs the last couple of weeks, here are the facts:

1. Peter has two younger brothers. Walker has two younger brothers.

2. Peter's mother goes on a date. Walker's mother is a widow who, I'm sure, dates (boys tell me she's considered a MILF).

3. Jake Soros punched Walker in the stomach today and he squeaked.

4. Nobody but Lina Ozu would be dopey enough to think a squeaky stomach is cute and then pretend it's a mouse and try to have a conversation with it.

5. It's typical Lina to think she's the only girl in school who's in love or has a decent boyfriend, and then to brag about it on her blog but pretend she's being all modest and not bragging about it, even though she is. Bragging, I mean.

Lina, you are so busted. Walker, I hope you like having your secrets spread all over school. Lina, you'd better hope he likes you a whole lot.

And, everybody, stop reading Mood Swing! Now that I've

shown you what a pack of lies it is. I mean, it's all true, but Peter and Tess are made up. Except that they're really Lina and Peter. You know what I mean.

"Ugh." The panicky taste had spread through Lina's whole mouth. She hoped Walker couldn't smell it on her breath. Stupid Autumn. She had ruined everything.

"I guess changing our names wasn't as good a disguise as I'd thought," Lina said.

"She pretty much nailed us," Walker said.

"I'm sorry," Lina said. "I'll stop writing about us. At least, no more super-personal stuff. Okay? I promise."

"Thank you." She could see the relief on Walker's face. His smile lost its tension and went back to being a sweet Walker smile. He forgave her so easily. It was wonderful.

But now what would she write about on Mood Swing? Without the juicy details of her dates with Walker, what did she have left? Covering the latest lacrosse game? Stiff, sterile dinners with her parents? Holly and Mads were usually good for a make-out story, but she couldn't tell their secrets in public or they'd be mad at her, too. What was she going to do?

6 After Dreck

I don't get it," Mads said. She and Lina and Holly were eating lunch at a table outside. Across the school courtyard, Quintana was sitting under the big elm tree with a senior named Holter Knapp. They were mauling each other.

"She's been here, what—a week?—and she's already hooked one of the cutest boys in school," Mads said. "And almost every boy at the Speed Dating party ranked her Extremely Attractive. One guy even called her Beyond the Realm of Feminine Allure. Whatever that means."

"She does have a good body," Lina said.

"Sebastiano says she has animal magnetism," Holly said. "She isn't shy, that's for sure. I heard she was making out with Nick Henin at the Pinetop last weekend."

"I still can't get into that stupid place," Mads said. The Pinetop Lounge was a local bar known for not carding minors—except for Mads, who was so young-looking, even the Pinetop wouldn't serve her.

Mads watched as Quintana and Holter broke apart for a second and smiled at each other as if they knew a secret. Then Quintana licked her lips. Holter moved his face toward hers, but she ducked her head away, just an inch out of reach, so he had to try again, move even closer. . . .

"Why is he so into her?" Mads said. "Do you think it's the lip-licking?"

"Stop watching them, Mads," Holly said. "It's not polite."

"Why not?" Mads said. "They're kissing right out in the open, in front of everybody. If they don't want people to watch, they can get a room."

"I can't watch and eat at the same time," Lina said, dropping her turkey sandwich.

But Mads couldn't tear her eyes away. Animal magnetism—she'd heard of that before. But what was it? Why was it so powerful? And how did you get it?

"She must be a great kisser," she said, more to herself than to anyone else. Quintana tilted up her chin, gave Holter's nose a quick lick, then twisted her head to the side. Holter closed his eyes. He looked as if he were in heaven.

I wonder what Stephen looks like when we're kissing? Mads thought. She didn't know because she usually had her eyes closed. (Did *he?*) But somehow she doubted he was in heaven. If you were in heaven, would you suddenly leave for some lame reason like something was poking your butt? No, you'd try to stay as long as you could no matter what, ignoring any silly distractions.

"I think I'll try some of Quintana's moves on Stephen," Mads said. "When it comes to kissing, I still feel like I don't know what I'm doing." She wished Stephen would walk by that minute so she could practice Quintana's techniques on him while they were fresh in her mind. But Stephen was a junior, and their schedules were completely at odds. They hardly ever saw each other at school. Kissing practice would have to wait until later.

"Maybe having some road-tested moves will give me confidence," Mads said. "And isn't that all you need? Confidence?"

She looked at Holly and Lina for confirmation. They looked doubtful.

"Confidence is good," Lina said.

"Skill can be helpful," Holly said.

"But confidence can't hurt," Lina said.

"Good luck with that," Holly said.

"Thanks," Mads said. Her brief spurt of confidence had completely evaporated. "Thanks a lot."

"What's that?" Mads pointed at a gigantic gray blob suspended from the ceiling. It was a long piece of stretchy gray fabric stuffed with something soft and tied at various points to make it puff in and out like a worm.

"That's one of Mom's new pieces," Stephen said. "It's supposed to be a small intestine. She's doing this series of sculptures called Internalize, where they're all body organs." He pointed to a curvy, brown-red cushion on the floor that Mads was about to sit on. "See, that's a kidney. And there's a halfway-finished heart in the corner. I think that's as far as she's gotten."

Mads quickly stepped away from the kidney. She knew better than to sit on people's sculpture, as long as they identified it for her.

She and Stephen had gone to a movie, but when it was over they still had a lot of night to kill, so he brought her to his mother's house. His mother was a sculptor. She was upstairs in her bedroom, reading. Stephen thought she'd pretty much leave them alone, but for extra privacy he'd led Mads out back to the art studio. It was attached to the kitchen by a short, enclosed walkway.

"Is that a couch, or a spleen?" Mads asked, pointing at a ratty blue velvet love seat.

"Couch," Stephen said. "Perfectly safe to sit on. Are you sure you don't want anything from the kitchen?"

"I'm sure," Mads said.

He sat beside her on the blue velvet love seat. He put his arm around her. She leaned against him.

"Maybe we shouldn't go out to the movies anymore," he said.

She sprang forward, shocked. "What do you mean?" Was this the introduction to a breakup speech? Why else would he suggest not going to the movies?

"I mean, at the theater," he said. "Most of the movies they show at the Twin are such a waste of time. Even the foreign flicks. What happened to German cinema? That movie we saw tonight was total dreck."

"Well, that *was* the title," Mads said.

"Okay, the title may have been *Dreck*, but it's not supposed to be literal garbage," Stephen said. "Or maybe it is. What do I know? Is Western culture declining that quickly?

I'm only sixteen and I'm already nostalgic for an earlier time. Where are the Fassbinders, the Wim Wenderses? The Werner Herzogs? The Weitz brothers?"

The who? Mads sat back and relaxed. He wasn't breaking up with her. He was just ranting. He did that sometimes.

"From now on we should just stay home and rent old movies," he said. "Nothing made after 1999. No, 2001. Okay, 2004. But nothing trashy, unless it's the good kind of trashy, like John Waters."

"That's all right with me," Mads said. She didn't care if they never saw another movie like *Dreck* again. Lots of German people running around Berlin wearing gorilla costumes. Except for this one guy who wore a Santa suit. At least, she thought it was a Santa suit. He had a red nose, and he was fat. The movie seemed like it was supposed to be funny, but Mads hadn't seen a funny German movie yet. Okay, she'd only seen three German movies in her whole life. But none of them were the least bit funny.

Mads wished he hadn't started talking about German cinema—it made her feel insecure. She didn't know anything about it. Stephen was kind of intellectual, but he wasn't snotty about it at all and never wanted to make her feel stupid. She knew that. Still, to try the Quintana makeout moves she needed confidence, and talking about

German cinema wasn't giving it to her.

"From now on, we'll only watch good movies at home, and if we don't like them, we'll turn them off and start reading," she said, trying to use a sexy voice. "Or else . . ." She nuzzled her nose against his cheek to let him know it was time to change the subject. He got the message.

"Or else we can find other ways to entertain ourselves," he said. She playfully licked his nose. He laughed and wiped off her spit.

Mads licked her lips three times, the way she'd seen Quintana do it, in preparation. Stephen moved toward her. She ducked her head. His chin knocked into her eye.

"Ow," she said.

"Are you okay?" he asked.

She rubbed her eye and nodded. "Fine, really."

They tried again. Mads tilted her chin up. She was afraid to duck her head now, so she just kept it where it was. Stephen came to meet her, and their lips locked.

Now we're talking, she thought. They were happily kissing. Her eyes were closed. She was tempted to peek to see if he looked as if he were in heaven, the way Holter had looked when kissing Quintana. But she didn't want to lose her concentration, so she kept her eyes closed.

They sank into the love seat. He lay under her,

holding her tight. His lips parted open, just a little. Mads flicked her tongue inside, licking his tongue the way she'd licked his nose. He flicked his tongue back. She drove hers in deeper. Then she felt his body get tense. He sat up, knocking her off him. His eyes were wide open. "Did you hear something?" he asked.

Mads listened. Some insects *chirruped* outside. Other than that, all was still. "No," she said.

"I thought I heard something," he said. "Like my mother. Not that I'm not allowed to fool around with a girl or anything, but I don't exactly want her *witnessing* it."

"I know what you mean," Mads said. She listened again. "But I don't think she's coming."

"Sometimes she comes downstairs for a cup of tea at night," he said. "Okay, sorry. False alarm."

"That's all right," Mads said. "I'm not wild about the idea of her witnessing us, either."

They got back down to it, but they had to start over again. Not from the very beginning, but from earlier, so they could work back up to the place they'd left off. But just when they got there, he sat up again.

"There! See! A noise!" he said.

Mads did hear a clicking sound this time. Like someone with very long toenails tapping toward them through the walkway from the kitchen.

"Does your mother need a pedicure?" Mads asked. She turned around to see. It was only the Costellos' shaggy sheepdog.

"Hey, boy," Stephen said. "It's Nietzsche."

"Gesundheit," Mads said.

"Ha-ha. I never get tired of that one."

She put her hand behind Stephen's head and kissed him. "See, it's not your mother. Now, where were we?"

Nietzsche padded closer and whined. "He's hungry," Stephen said.

"Just ignore him," Mads said. "We can feed him later."

The dog whined again. He licked Mads' toes.

"Ick," she said.

Stephen stood up. "I've got to feed him. He won't leave us alone until I do."

Mads sighed and followed Stephen into the kitchen. Was there a problem here? She huffed into her palm and sniffed it, checking her breath. Smelled okay to her. You can't always tell if your own breath smells bad, because you're used to it, but Mads had gotten pretty good at detecting foulness.

After feeding the dog, Stephen noticed it was almost Mads' curfew time and said he'd better get her home. So that was it.

Is something wrong with me? Mads wondered. Weren't

boys supposed to be dying to get into your pants? So why did Stephen keep stopping just when things got hot?

Was it him? *No,* she thought. *It's got to be me. These things are always my fault.*

Then she remembered Quintana, her confidence, her breeziness, and scolded herself. Would Quintana let a lousy kiss get her down? (Would this happen to her in the first place? No, but never mind.) *Confidence! Stop blaming yourself!*

But if it wasn't her fault, it was his. And that meant she had a lousy boyfriend. Or, the third alternative: they had no chemistry. Also unacceptable. She couldn't win.

At least if it's my fault, she thought, *I can do something about it. And I will.*

7 A Message from Speed Racer

To:	hollygolitely
From:	your daily horoscope

HERE IS TODAY'S HOROSCOPE: CAPRICORN: Your heart is like a soccer ball—getting kicked around. Unfortunately, these days that's the only way you'll score.

"Why hasn't he called?" Holly moaned. "Why hasn't he e-mailed?"

Sebastiano had found her alone at Vineland after school and sat down to cheer her up. It had been almost a week since the Speed Dating party, and she couldn't stop thinking about Eli. She was obsessed with him. She'd only lasted two days before breaking her promise to herself and sending him an e-mail. She'd tried to keep it light, coy. Mysterious, like him. But how mysterious can you be when you're contacting someone who hasn't contacted you? The writing is on the wall, so to speak. Or the screen. Obviously, if you're communicating, you're interested.

Sebastiano broke out his BlackBerry and handed it to Holly. "Show me what you wrote him," he said.

Holly logged on to her e-mail and opened her SENT MAIL file. "Here."

Her e-mail said:

To: eli_eli_o
From: hollygolitely
Re: Speed Dating
Eli— How did you like the Speed Dating party? Lina, Mads,
and I are writing to everyone who participated to see if
they have any suggestions for making it better next
time. So, any suggestions?

This whole first paragraph was a total lie. Lina, Mads, and Holly didn't write to any of the other Speed Daters. Eli was the only one whose suggestions were solicited.

I'm Holly, by the way—the blonde in the middle of the table?
#8? I don't know if you remember me. We met at 3:17?

P.M.? Anyway, write back if you have any suggestions. Your input is greatly appreciated! —Holly Anderson, RSAGE

"That's your idea of coy?" Sebastiano frowned.

"God, I know, it's so lame," Holly said. "How could I have written something so stupid? No wonder he hasn't written back."

"You can always hold another Speed Dating thingy," Sebastiano said. "You will do it again, won't you? The last one was as good as *Desperate Housewives*, only more like Desperate High Schoolers. Which isn't saying much, but in this town, you get your jollies where you can."

"For you, maybe. You didn't have to suffer through it."

"Exactly."

"Next time, I'm staying out of it," Holly said. "I'll just sit with you and watch."

"Oh, no, you're not. You're going to go through the whole thing again and meet a nice shot of testosterone to take your mind off this little dweeb you're stuck on. Who looks exactly like Speed Racer, by the way. Which is funny, since you met him Speed Dating. I think I'll call him Speed from now on. Too bad you don't look much like Trixie. Maybe that's why you haven't heard from him."

"Shut up. He doesn't look like Speed Racer."

"Sure, he does. Those big, round, doe-like eyes. Anime eyes. And his thatch of black hair and trim little figure—"

"Stop it. He's not a cartoon character."

"Maybe not to you. But if you learned to see him that way, you wouldn't be so miserable."

Holly went limp in her chair, her head falling back, her hands pressed against her eyes. "I don't want a nice shot of testosterone. I want *him*! What is his story? Why does he have to be so friggin' mysterious?"

"That's it, get up," Sebastiano said. He rose.

"What?"

"Come on. I've heard enough. We're going for a ride, sister."

Holly got up, glad to be bossed around for the moment. "Where?"

"Let's take a little spin around old Griffith, shall we? Give me your keys."

"I'm not letting you drive my car."

"You're in no condition to drive. You're drunk on misery. Let's go."

"He's cute." Sebastiano pointed to a quarterback type walking down the path with a girl clinging to his midsection. "Why don't you go after him?"

"He's not my type," Holly said. "And he's taken."

"Hmm. Too bad." Sebastiano spun Holly's yellow VW Beetle through the green, manicured, winding paths of Griffith Academy, Eli's school. That was all she knew about him: his name, his e-mail address, and his school.

"Do they have a fencing team here?" Sebastiano asked. "Because Speed definitely looks like the fencing type to me. Muscular, yet slight. Possibly wrestling, but for your sake, I hope not."

"Why not wrestling?"

"You have no idea what those guys do to their bodies," Sebastiano said. "They're more weight-obsessed than a bulimic girl. Truly. They're sickos."

"Hmm. Sebastiano, what is the point of this little road trip?"

"Information-gathering," Sebastiano said. "To see if we can find out something useful about Mr. Racer. A clue. Does he have a girlfriend? Does he have any friends at all? Is he some kind of weirdo? You know, spying?"

They followed the small, tasteful signs to the gym. School was out for the day, so if Eli was around, he was probably doing a sport or after-school activity.

"What if he sees us?" Holly asked.

"Duck. And if he still sees you, lie."

Sebastiano pulled into a parking spot. Holly made a move to get out of the car, just as the gym door opened and a group of kids poured out. She quickly shut the car door and slouched low in her seat.

"There he is," Sebastiano said. Holly watched Eli. The sight of him made her heart race. She hadn't seen him in almost a week, and her memory of his looks had begun to fade. Except for his labyrinth eyes. Those, she'd never forget.

His hair was wet, as if he'd just taken a shower. So he did play some kind of sport. And he was surrounded by a mixed group of guys and girls, also wet-haired.

"Uh-oh. Girlfriend at six o'clock," Sebastiano said.

A girl approached the group, which fell away, leaving Eli alone with her. She jingled her keys at him. He grinned and snatched them away. Holly was seized with an urge to be that girl. Either to be her, or blow her away.

"That's it," Holly said. "He's got a girlfriend. I'll start erasing him from my mind right now. Can we stop off for some Chocolate Brainwash?"

"Not so fast," Sebastiano said. "I don't think she's a girlfriend. They haven't kissed, not even a peck. And look." Eli and the girl walked through the parking lot and got into a car. Eli drove. He pulled out, and Holly saw, printed on the back of the car, the words STUDENT DRIVER.

"I wish my driving instructor had been that cute," Sebastiano said.

"Me, too," Holly said. "So what if she's his driving teacher? He could still fall for her!"

"Trixie, calm down. Look, you've done what you can. If he's really your soul mate, he'll call. Or e-mail. And if he doesn't, he's not. And you'll be lucky you didn't waste months and months trying to mold him into soul mate material when he never was in the first place. So relax and let fate take its course. Okay?"

"Okay," Holly said, but she wasn't a "let fate take its course" type. And, for that matter, neither was Sebastiano.

"If you ever fall in love, you are going to be so screwed," Holly said. "I'm going to throw all your truisms and bad advice right back at you."

"There, there," Sebastiano said as he drove through the plush Griffith campus. "I'll ask around and see if anybody knows anything about the guy. Happy?"

"No," Holly said. "Not until I've solved Eli like a puzzle. He's going to be mine or I'm going to know why not."

"Ugh, you girls are so hopeless," Sebastiano said. "When are you going to realize guys aren't mysterious at all? They're just big lumps. You only think they're mysterious because you can't believe a human being can be nothing but a big lump, but trust me, they can, and half of them are. The boy half. And they're proud of it."

"What about you? Are you nothing but a big lump?"

"You'd better believe it, sister. The biggest."

That shut Holly up. She had to admit he sounded proud of it.

She checked her in-box one last time before going to bed that night. And there it was. Blinking like a ruby, an unopened treasure.

To: hollygolitely
From: eli_eli_o
Re: 3:17

Forgive me, Holly. I've thought of nothing but you since we met
last Saturday. But I was afraid to make a move. I knew
that once I did, once I made a move in your direction,
that would be that. My fate would be sealed. I could
never go back. My search for love would be over. I didn't
think I was ready. But my heart didn't care. Every day at
3:17 it beat for you. And tomorrow is Saturday. My heart
overruled my head. It moved my fingers and made me
write to you. I knew if I lost you, I'd never forgive myself.
And so, sweet Holly, if you could see me now, you would see
a piece of clay, waiting for your hands to reach out and
mold it into a work of art. Say you'll be my divine potter.
—Eli

It was beyond anything she could have hoped for. He hadn't written because he liked her too much, and was afraid. She saved the e-mail, then printed it out, just to be safe. She wanted to keep it forever. Her first e-mail from her soul mate.

8 Midnight Rendezvous with Squeaky

To:	linaonme
From:	your daily horoscope

HERE IS TODAY'S HOROSCOPE: CANCER: You will violate your usual policy of not fraternizing with the enemy, which will remind you why you had that policy in the first place.

Did you read Mood Swing today?"

Lina overheard Claire Kessler and Ingrid Bauman talking in the gym locker room. They were in the showers, and Lina was waiting for a stall to become available. Ingrid and Claire were rather moronically shouting over the steam as if nobody could hear them.

"Yeah, but I'm not going to read it anymore after

today," Ingrid said. "It's just not as good without Peter and Tess."

"I know, it's boring," Claire said. "Who cares about that new girl, Quintana Rhea? We can see what she's doing with our own eyes. We don't need to read about it on the Internet."

"Yeah, you can see what she's up to whether you want to or not," Ingrid said. "Slurp slurp."

"Lina obviously has no gossip sources. Pete and Tess were totally her and Walker, and she doesn't know any dirt about anybody but herself. So she has no dirt. End of story."

"End of Mood Swing," Ingrid said. "No dirt, no readers."

Ingrid stepped out of the shower, wrapping a towel around her. "All yours," she said to Lina.

"You know, I heard everything you said," Lina said.

"Good. No point in deluding yourself," Ingrid said.

Lina sighed and stepped into the shower. Ingrid was a bitch, but she was right. Lina had no dirt. And that was what the people wanted. But she just wasn't a dirt-digging type, not when it came to gossip. She didn't mind digging up muckraker dirt, the kind of digging that was an investigative reporter's job. She didn't mind picking up on the odd juicy sound bite. But she had too much respect for people's privacy to betray their confidences and publish their secrets. Now that she couldn't publish her own secrets, she had nothing.

"Are you guys going to do another Speed Dating party?" Autumn asked. She surprised Lina by slipping into the stacks at the library and whispering into her ear. They were in the same history class and were supposed to be doing research for a paper.

"Yeah, probably," Lina said. "Why?" Autumn had a boyfriend, Vince Overbeck, whom she was crazy about. Or so she always said. Lina, Mads, and Holly had made the match themselves, through the Dating Game. So why would Autumn be interested in Speed Dating?

"Eh, I'm having doubts about Vince," Autumn said. "Do you ever think he's—I don't know—boring? I mean, I noticed recently that he doesn't say much."

This was why Autumn, a blabber, had liked him in the first place. Lina was surprised she'd stopped talking long enough to notice.

"Just because he doesn't say much doesn't mean he's boring," Lina said. "I wouldn't rush to break up with him, Autumn. It's not pretty out there."

"Oh, come on," Autumn said. "You've got it good with Walker, right? I heard about the other night. . . ."

"The other night?" Something *had* happened with

Walker a few nights earlier, but how would Autumn know about it?

"He told me. Don't look so surprised! Who do you think is his main source for inside dope on the girls' lacrosse team?"

"It's just—he never mentioned telling anyone—"

"Why would he? Anyway, it was so sexy! How did it happen?"

"The other night?" Lina said. "You mean, when I sneaked him into my house?"

"On a school night?" Autumn said.

"My parents won't let him come over on school nights," Lina said. "And my mother is extra vigilant since she found his boxers in the bathroom."

"Oh, yeah—what happened with that?"

"I told her they were mine," Lina said. "But I'm not sure she believed me."

"So how did you sneak Walker into your house?"

"My room's on the first floor, so he knocked on the patio door. I almost had a heart attack."

"I bet! I would have freaked. You probably thought he was a serial killer, right?" Autumn asked.

"Just for a second. It was almost midnight. My parents were in bed. So I let him in and we watched TV with the sound down."

"See, I've never done anything like that with Vince," Autumn said. "Of course, my parents aren't psychotically overprotective like yours, so if he wanted to come over, he could and it wouldn't be a problem. Still, it's more exciting this way, right? So basically, he spent the night at your house. And your parents had no idea?"

"Well, it was an accident. We fell asleep in front of the TV. Thank god I woke up at five. He sneaked out before my parents got up for work and caught us."

"I guess you guys fooled around a lot between midnight and five in the morning, am I right?"

"Well, a little . . ."

"I'm so jealous," Autumn said. "See, I need a guy like that. All Vince does is tell me how beautiful I am and how much he loves me. It's gets old, it really does."

"I don't know," Lina said. "I wouldn't mind. I'm afraid Walker thinks my butt is too fat."

"What? You're crazy," Autumn said. "It's not fat at all. Why, did he say that?"

"No," Lina said. "But he's always telling me he likes my face and my hair and my arms and my legs and my chest and my stomach and my feet, but he never mentions my butt."

Autumn shook her head. "That does make you wonder."

Lina had never had a conversation like this with

Autumn before. It felt strange.

"But no one could ever think your butt was fat, Lina," Autumn said. "So just put that out of your mind!"

"Psst! Autumn! Are you back here?" Ingrid's face appeared through the books on the other side of the stack.

"Whoops! Gotta go!" Autumn hurried away with Ingrid, leaving Lina to wonder what that was all about. And she didn't come up with an answer. But the more she turned the incident over in her mind, the more nervous she got.

Mood Swing
Current Mood: Wondering . . .

The first Speed Dating party at Vineland was a big success. At least two new matches have come out of it, which is good news. There were lots of kids from other schools there—did seeing the competition help light a fire under your butts, boys? Whatever it was, the social scene at RSAGE is finally cooking. New blood. A certain Miss Cue is very busy—my sources have spotted her making out with two RSAGE seniors and a Draper boy. Not all at the same time.

Let's see, what else . . .

She paused, trying to come up with something juicy

to write, but all she could think about was herself and Walker. For inspiration, she checked her mailbox.

To: moodswingmistress
From: magicgirl
Bring back Pete and Tess! Mood swing sucks without them!

From: gorgon3
What did Tess's parents do after her mother found the
    underpants? Was she grounded? Did they yell at Pete?
    Did Tess lie? I must know!

From: x-static
Where are Tess and Pete???? What have you done with
    them??? bring them back, you murderer!!!!

From: rangerred
I have Pete's underpants. I'm holding them hostage until you
    tell us what happened to Pete and Tess! Why must you
    torture me?

Okay, so the kids missed the old column. *Surely,* Lina thought, *an adult would appreciate the new, responsible Mood Swing.* She couldn't resist checking in with Erica for a reaction.
    To: ehoward

From: linaonme
Re: mood swing
Dear Erica,
I've revamped my column a little—just wanted to let you
     know. What do you think?
Lina Ozu

To: linaonme
From: ehoward
Re: mood swing
Lina—Just a quick response off the top of my head. What
     happened to Peter and Tess? They had such a sweet
     little love thing going. I was kind of hooked on it. And
     what you wrote about them was juicier than the stuff in
     the new column. . . .
Erica

Great, Lina thought. *Everybody hates my blog now. And on
top of that, I could lose the internship!*

Maybe if she explained it to Erica, it would help her
case.

To: ehoward
From: linaonme
Re: mood swing

Erica—I'm glad you liked the characters of Peter and Tess. Unfortunately, they were pseudonyms for real people, and the kids at my school figured out who they were, and they were embarrassed, especially Peter . . . so I had to stop writing about them. It was too personal and revealing. I think I learned a valuable lesson in journalistic responsibility. So from now on, I'm going to put only well-substantiated news on my blog. No more gossip. I'm sure you'll find it just as interesting as all that trivia about Peter and Tess.

Lina

To: linaonme
From: ehoward
Re: mood swing

Lina—I'm glad to see you grappling with lessons on journalistic responsibility. It's important. But don't forget you have a responsibility to your audience, too—and it never hurts to keep them interested and entertained!

Erica

She's right, Lina thought. *Everybody is right.* Mood Swing just wasn't as good when it was clean and responsible. But what could she do? It wasn't worth losing Walker over it. She'd just have to find another way to be entertaining.

Nuclear Autumn: Keeping You Informed of the Latest Developments in the Life of Autumn Nelson

All right, sweeties! You want the dirt on "Peter" and "Tess"? We got it right here! And it's another killer. Those two just can't keep their hands off each other! I guess they can't go one day without the lovin' because Pete actually sneaked over to Tess's house—on a school night—after her parents went to bed. I got this direct from Tess herself, so you know it's the real deal. Tess is taking big risks here. Her parents are already tetchy after the underpants incident—which, by the way, she cleverly handled by telling her mother they were hers, even though they're too big for her. She tried to convince Mom that boys' boxers are the latest spring fashion for girls. Not sure if Mom bought it—how dumb could she be? But it kept her quiet for now.

Tess likes to live on the edge. She let Pete into her room and they stayed up half the night watching TV with the sound down low and her parents twenty feet away! Must have been hard to keep it down, what with him squeaking all over the place every time you look cross-eyed at him.

They were so blasé, they actually fell asleep in front of the TV, and Tess had to hustle Pete out of the house when her father got up for work. They came this close to getting caught. Those two lovebirds! What will they come up with next—doing it on the table in the lunchroom? Can't wait to hear that—squeak squeak!

Maybe not. There may be trouble in paradise, after all, kids. Tess confessed that she's afraid Pete thinks her butt is fat. I'm not saying it is or it isn't, but it just goes to show that we all have our insecurities! And even the hottest couple has their little problems. I predict this butt issue will blow up in their faces by the end of the school year. What's your prediction? Write me! Give me feedback!

Look to Nuclear Autumn as your only source on all things Pete and Tess! More news later in the week!

"Oh, my god," Mads said.

"Oh, my god," Holly said.

"That little bitch," Lina said.

They were in the library during study hall. The buzz in the halls about Peter and Tess had driven them to the computer to look up Nuclear Autumn, the source of the rumors.

"How did she find all this out?" Mads asked.

"I told her myself," Lina said. "Right here in the library. She was being friendly and she made it sound as if Walker had already told her everything. But I filled in all the details for her, like an idiot. God, Walker is going to kill me! But, first, I think I'll play field hockey with her head."

Mads looked toward the library door and gulped. "Uh-oh."

Lina knew before she even turned her head. Walker.

"Here comes Squeaky," Mads said.

His face was stony. "Lina, can I talk to you for a minute. Alone?"

"It's not your fault," Holly whispered. "Don't let him take it out on you."

"Yeah, the two of you should gang up on Autumn," Mads said. "Bond in your anti-Autumn-ness. Use it to make your relationship stronger."

"Good luck," Holly said.

Lina walked out of the library with Walker. He cornered her against a locker.

"I thought we said no more sharing our secrets with the whole school."

"I know," Lina said. "I never meant for this to happen. I'm furious with Autumn! She tricked me! We were just talking girl-to-girl. I had no idea she was going to post everything I said!"

"God, I can't believe you girls," Walker said. "Why did you have to tell her anything at all? You don't even like her."

"I told you, she tricked me," Lina said. "She made it sound like you had told her everything. She said she's your source for lacrosse news."

"She did? That little liar! Well, I have talked to her

once or twice about their goalie problems . . . but that's not the same as telling her I slept over at your house."

"I know, Walker. I'm really sorry. I won't tell her anything else—I promise. Her source on Peter and Tess has dried up. She'll have to find somebody else to gossip about now."

"I hope so," Walker said. "I'm sorry I got so mad at you, Lina." He pressed his forehead against hers. "It was kind of fun to wake up next to you that morning. Lying on the cold, hard floor with a blanket tangled around us and the sofa cushions under our heads. . . ."

"Yeah, it was fun, wasn't it?"

They kissed. It was a definite make-up kiss. He had forgiven her.

9 N-n-n-naked

HERE IS TODAY'S HOROSCOPE: VIRGO: You are on a search for wisdom. At least, you should be.

Round Two," Mads said. She and Lina were setting up the second Speed Dating party at Vineland. Holly had begged off, claiming her mother needed help getting ready for a dinner party that night.

"I don't believe that for a second," Lina said. "She hates helping her mother."

"I don't believe it, either," Mads said. "She's chicken."

"Can't face her adoring public," Lina said.

"She only likes *E-li,*" Mads said. Mads and Lina had tried to convince Holly that another Speed Dating party might bring another soul mate, but Holly insisted that you can't have more than one at a time.

The partyers trickled in and took their seats at the long table in the garden. Mads quivered at the sight of Sean in seat #3. She'd quivered when she had seen his name on the sign-up list. She'd quivered when she had seen him at school. She'd quivered when she'd heard his name. He made her quiver, that's all there was to it.

Quintana slinked into a seat near the end of the table. "I can't believe she's back for more," Lina whispered to Mads. "She got at least four dates out of the last party."

"I know," Mads said. "Speed Dating works really well for her."

"How many dates does a girl need?" Lina said. "Do you think she does it for the ego rush? Being constantly reminded that so many boys like her?"

Mads had wondered about this herself, and come to a different conclusion. "I think she's an idealist. She's looking for her ideal guy, and she doesn't want to rule anyone out. So she has to meet as many guys as possible."

"Did she say that?"

"No," Mads said. "It's my theory. Is everyone here?"

"We're missing Girl #15," Lina said. She checked the

sign-up list for the one name not checked in. "Gia Gersh."

"Check your cell," Mads said. "Maybe she called to say she's running late."

Lina checked her phone. "There's a message." She listened for a few seconds. "She's not coming," Lina said. "She's home puking her guts out. Stomach flu."

"What are we going to do?" Mads asked. "Now we have an extra boy. They'll have to take turns sitting for six minutes with no one to talk to and nothing to do."

"Unless you take Gia's place," Lina said.

"Me? Why me? I have a boyfriend."

"You don't have to date any of the guys," Lina said. "Just talk to them. So they won't feel ripped off."

"Why don't you do it?" Mads asked.

"Because Walker's meeting me here later and it would be weird if he saw me," Lina said.

"I guess," Mads said. Stephen wouldn't come near the Speed Dating parties. He'd said he was afraid the hormone surge would give him vicarious acne. "I'll have to tell the boys up front that I have a boyfriend and I won't date them."

"Just be nice to them," Lina said. "We don't want bad word of mouth. Do it for the good of the blog."

"All right." Mads took the last empty seat, at the end of the table next to Quintana. She'd be able to watch

Quintana in action. And, of course, she'd get six minutes with Sean.

"Hey, girl," Quintana said. "What are you doing here?"

"Filling in for a sick Speed Dater," Mads said.

"Well, don't steal any cute ones away from me," Quintana said.

"I don't think you have to worry about that," Mads said.

"Everybody ready?" Lina asked. "Go!"

Mads focused on the boy in front of her. Alex Sipress. She knew him from school. In fact, she'd hung out with him once at a party at Sean's house. She'd been tipsy that night. Okay, drunk. Okay, she'd puked. In Sean's mother's room.

"We meet again, Octopussy," Alex said. "I already know the short but sweet story of your life. Want to go out one night?"

"I can't," Mads said. "I have a boyfriend."

"So what are you doing here?"

"Filling in for a sick girl. I'm just entertaining you until you go to the next person."

"Oh."

Mads didn't know what to say next. Entertaining fifteen boys for six minutes each was not going to be easy.

They sat quietly. It was awkward. In the silence,

Mads heard Quintana say, "I like excitement, but it's like a drug. You've got to keep upping the dose, doing more and more risky things. . . ."

The boy she was talking to listened, rapt, practically bouncing in his seat.

"That guy wants to leap over the table and jump on top of her," Alex said. "Right now."

"Yeah," Mads said.

"Do I get her next?" Alex asked.

"No. You have to go around to the other end of the table and work your way down. You get Quintana last."

"Is that good or bad?"

"Depends. Probably good. You'll be the last guy she sees, so she'll remember you best."

"Awesome."

"Time!" Lina called. "Everybody switch."

Alex got to his feet. "Thanks for killing six minutes with me."

Quintana's boy moved into the seat across from Mads. Mads studied him. He was short, chubby, with pale brown hair. He wore a Giants T-shirt. His looks were unmemorable, except for the beads of sweat on his upper lip. Mads hoped for his sake he had a killer personality.

"Hi, I'm Dave. So what's exciting about you?"

What's exciting about you? she wanted to ask. "You know

what?" she said. "Nothing is exciting about me. Why don't we just sit here and listen to the people next to us talking? You don't mind, do you?"

"Her?" Dave nodded at Quintana. "I could listen to her talk all day. But preferably all night."

"You're witty, Dave," Mads said. "Too bad I already have a boyfriend."

Dave gave her a funny look, as if there might be something wrong with her. Then they turned their attention to Quintana. Mads hoped she and her boy, Jason, would be so into each other, they wouldn't realize they were being eavesdropped on.

"Of course I take showers when I have to," Quintana said. "When I'm in a hurry or after gym or whatever. But I really love a good, long soak in the bath. With almond-scented oil, that's my favorite. Just lie back, naked, the sun streaming in through the window, making me all warm. . . ."

Did Quintana know what she was doing to this guy? His mouth hung slack as he absorbed what she said. A drop of saliva appeared at the corner of his lip, grew bigger, then dripped down his chin.

"You'd think she was talking about food," Mads said.

"From now on, I'm switching to baths," Dave said.

"Jason, why are you staring at me like that?" Quintana said. "Just because I said the word 'naked'?"

"N-n-n-naked," Jason stammered.

Let me try that, Mads thought. She tapped Dave's hand to get his attention. "Hey. Dave. Listen to this." She paused, licked her lips for maximum effect. *"Naked."*

Dave didn't seem to hear her. He was still mesmerized by Quintana. Mads tapped him again. He turned toward her groggily. "Huh?"

"Did you hear me? I said *naked.*"

"What? Yeah. Is time up yet?"

Mads sighed. Why didn't it work for her? Was it her voice? Her intonation? The context?

"Time's up!" Lina called.

Dave got up to leave. "Uh, I've got to—" He walked away without finishing the sentence. It was as if his mind had melted.

"Nice knowing you, Dave," Mads called after him.

"I'm bored," Quintana said as the next boy took his place.

"You don't seem bored," Mads said.

"Don't I?" She frowned. "These boys don't have much to say, do they? I'm doing all the talking!"

She turned to her new partner. "Is it hot today? Or is it me?" She pulled her sweater over her head, leaving only a white tank top. "There. That's better. Now, who are you?" She reached across the table and smoothed the boy's rumpled shirt so she could read his name tag. "Jason. I just had one of those." She glanced at the first Jason, who was now sitting across from Mads but still riveted to Quintana. "Are all Jasons as good-looking as you two?"

Mads sat through more of this, boy after boy after boy, making mental notes, until Sean finally reached the chair across from Quintana. Mads told her boy—nameless, faceless, at this point she hardly cared who he was—to sit down and be quiet if he knew what was good for him. She didn't want to miss a word of the Sean-Quintana bout.

Quintana: Hi, Sean.

Sean: Hi, Quin. Tana. Anyone call you Quin?

Quintana: Sure. My family. Old friends. But what are you doing here? I thought you were taken.

Sean: Hey, I'm not married. Anyway, Jane's pissing me off. She's been hanging with this college dude, so I thought I'd make her jealous.

Quintana: Oh. Well, how's it working so far?

Sean: Not so good. Till now.

Quintana: I'm not sure I want to be used to make another girl jealous.

Sean: Then I won't. I'll dump Jane altogether if you'll go out with me.

Quintana: Just once? You'd dump your girlfriend for one date with me?

Sean: That's what I said. You in?

Quintana: Well . . . okay. Why not.

Sean: Excellent. I've got another date this Friday, but she's got a curfew. What if I pick you up afterward, say, eleven?

Quintana: You'll dump your girlfriend, but you won't cancel your date with another girl?

Sean: You're right. I can always see that girl another night.

Lina: Time!

Sean: See you Friday?

Quintana: I'll think about it.

Sean: Okay. You think about it, and I'll see you Friday.

He moved over to Mads. He was the first boy of the day who didn't have to be forced to drag himself away from Quintana. He grinned at Mads and said, "Hey, kid. Paint any pictures of me lately?"

Quiver. "Not lately," Mads said. "I've been doing animal portraits. But if you feel like posing, I could draw you again."

"Maybe. My mom says she wants a portrait of me for the living room. But I think she means a professional portrait. No offense."

"Oh."

"Not that you're not a good artist or anything. Just . . . you know."

"Sure."

Sean looked around, scanned the table, and got up. "Well, I really just came to this thing for a kick, see who'd show up, you know. I got what I wanted out of it. Think I'll split. Later."

"Later."

He walked away from the table with a wave to Alex and another to Quintana. Now there were more girls than boys at the party. Mads was no longer needed as a place-holder. She got up and joined Lina at the head table.

"Learn anything?" Lina asked.

"Yes," Mads said. "I learned that boys really, really like Quintana."

"You already knew that."

"I know," Mads said. "But now I've got a PhD in it."

10 Absorbing the Moonbeams

HERE IS TODAY'S HOROSCOPE: CAPRICORN: Life is full of
mysteries. Why should today be any different?

How did you find this restaurant?" Holly asked.
It was Friday night, their first date, and Eli had
brought her to a tiny Mexican place in Santa
Marta. Santa Marta was about an hour's drive from Carlton
Bay, and even smaller. The restaurant, Lucia's, sat on a cliff
overlooking the ocean. It was dark and candlelit and dec-
orated with Mexican handicrafts. "It's very romantic,"
Holly added.

"Oh, I have an interest in Mexico, and Mexican

things," Eli said. He tapped his fork against hers so it made a *ting*. "The candlelight turns your hair into gold."

Holly self-consciously touched her hair. "Thank you."

She couldn't believe this night had finally come. She'd been thinking about him so much since the Speed Dating party, imagining his face, trying to guess what he would say to her if they were alone together. Which wasn't easy, since he hadn't given her much to go on the first time they'd met. And he'd taken so long to get in touch with her, it made her uneasy. Yes, he said he was afraid he'd fall in love with her too quickly, but Holly's fake-o-meter buzzed slightly at that excuse, as much as she wanted to believe it. Still, what choice did she have but to meet with him, then wait and see?

"Tell me about yourself," Eli said. "I want to know everything."

"Hmm," Holly said. "Where should I start? The creature that is Holly has many lives, many moods, many facets."

"I can see that," Eli said. "Tell about your family. Do you have any brothers or sisters? What are your parents like?"

"I have an older sister, Piper. She's a freshman at Stanford. We get along okay when she doesn't pull her Queen Bee trip on me. We get along better than ever now that she's away at school."

"Is she beautiful like you?"

"She looks different from me, more like my mom. I think she's prettier. She's really thin, and her hair's darker than mine, and she has freckles. She's cool-looking."

"And your parents?"

"Curt and Jen? They're okay. They don't bother me too much. My dad likes to tease me sometimes. They go to a lot of parties and dinners. They pretty much let me do what I want."

"You're so lucky," Eli said. "My family has me in a dynastic stranglehold."

"A what?"

"I don't blame them. It's only because there's so much at stake. My father has a ranch down in Santa Barbara. He left us two years ago to live there."

"So your parents split up, huh? Sometimes I think mine should. Just get it over with, you know?"

"No, you shouldn't wish for that," Eli said. "Trust me, it's a terrible thing when it happens. My mother—I probably shouldn't say this, but my mother has been addicted to painkillers ever since."

"That's terrible," Holly said. "She must have been so hurt when he left."

"Well, yes, she was hurt when he left, but the stab wounds didn't help, either."

Holly gasped. "Stab wounds? What are you talking about?"

"My poor mother," Eli said. "She's had to have a lot of surgery ever since . . . ever since Imelda stabbed her with her own diamond-studded stilettos."

Holly needed a moment to take this in. "Stilettos? As in shoes?"

"Yes."

"Your mother wears diamond-studded shoes?"

"She's very flamboyant," Eli said. "But then, so is Imelda."

"Who's Imelda?"

"She was our maid. Now she's my stepmother."

"Your father had an affair with her?"

Eli nodded. "She's very greedy. She wanted to marry my father, so she tried to kill my mother. My father took her away, partly to save my mother's life. Now my mother's a basket case. She can walk, but she prefers the wheel-chair."

"Wow," Holly said. "That's some family story."

"I know. More sangria?"

He poured the fruity punch into Holly's glass. Holly picked out an orange segment and sucked on it. No wonder Eli had acted so strangely. His background was pretty weird.

"What about brothers and sisters?" she asked. "Do you have any?"

Eli looked away. "That's very complicated. I'll explain it to you some other time." His eyes returned to settle on her face. "Right now all I want to do is drink you in, like this sangria. *Salud.*"

They clinked glasses. She felt herself getting lost again in the gray-green-gold labyrinth of his eyes. *What am I getting myself into?* she wondered. Whatever it was, it wouldn't be dull. She could feel herself perched on the edge of an adventure.

After dinner, they got into his car, a blue Honda, and drove south along the coastline. Holly had been surprised when he offered to pick her up; since spying on him with Sebastiano and spotting him in the student driver car, she'd thought he didn't have his license yet. But it turned out he'd just gotten his driver's license, even though he was already seventeen. He might have been on his way to take his driving test the day she had seen him.

Just outside of Carlton Bay, they pulled into an over-look and stopped to watch the moon over the water. They got out of the car and sat on the rocks, side by side. Eli didn't say much, and he didn't touch her, didn't reach for her hand, didn't start petting her hair the way so many boys did. He simply sat still and stared at the moon. Holly did the same, stealing sidelong glances at him from time to time. What was his story? She knew some of it, the lurid family parts, but that wasn't what she meant. What did he want from her? Where did he think this was all going, if anywhere?

"I like to sit outside and kind of absorb the moonlight," he said at last. "I can feel it sinking into my body through my skin and my eyes. I feel like it gives me some kind of special power."

"Power to do what?" Holly asked.

"I don't know," Eli said. "But I think I've absorbed enough moon rays for tonight. Ready to go?"

He stood up and held out his hand. She took it, and he helped her to her feet. They returned to the car and drove home. A CD was playing, the Shins. The music filled the car, so that there was no need to talk. Holly had the feeling the Shins were doing all their talking for them, much more beautifully than they could do it themselves.

He pulled up in front of her house. She looked at him. He looked at her. He leaned forward.

Here we go, Holly thought. *No guy can make it through a whole evening without trying some sort of pass.*

He pressed his lips against hers, softly. Then he pulled back. "Good night," he said. "I had a beautiful night."

That was it? She held still for a moment to make sure he didn't want to suddenly start mauling her. She wouldn't have minded, not much.

But he just smiled. So she said, "I had a beautiful night, too, Eli. Thank you." She opened the car door and said, "Good night," before shutting it. He waited while she walked along the stone path to her front door. She opened the door and waved. He blinked his headlights, then drove off.

That was the sexiest kiss I've ever had, she thought as she leaned against the door. The energy from his lips still buzzed on hers, like that lip gloss that stings and is supposed to give you a puffier pout. Maybe it was the moon's energy she felt in that kiss.

He was a little weird. She knew that. And from what she'd heard so far, his family was beyond dysfunctional. But none of that mattered. He was Eli. She'd met him at 3:17. And she was a goner.

11 Dissection

To:	linaonme
From:	your daily horoscope

HERE IS TODAY'S HOROSCOPE: CANCER: You're perfectly happy sitting alone with a good book. This will come in handy when your social life withers away to nothing.

Mood Swing
Current Mood: Don't ask

The third Speed Dating party was held at Vineland last Saturday, and scored another big success. Though this time, the crowd that signed up was a little different from before. The first two groups of Speed Daters were, for the most part, a fairly conventional crew. This time about half the participants were hardcore Goths, punks, or otherwise misfits. Interesting. But it worked.

One guy, a Draper student who shall remain nameless (because I can't remember what his name was), showed up sporting a David Bowie Spiders from Mars look, complete with dyed-blond hair, space-blue spandex over a cadaverous frame, and a lightning bolt painted over one eye on his chalky face. At the first Speed Dating party he might have been a reject, but this time he had the Goth chicks swooning. A certain Rosewood Poetess was especially smitten, though she didn't want to admit it. When her six minutes were up and she faced the prospect of losing David Bowie to a girl with a safety pin in her cheek, and the next boy in line was a yucky freshman wearing a cape, she decided to stop playing by the rules. She dug in and refused to let David Bowie go on to the next girl. "He's mine for the rest of the party," she declared. "You in the cape—go around me."

Safety Pin Girl refused to go along with this, and who can blame her? David Bowie was definitely the catch of this crowd, and Cape Boy the dud. True to her punk ethics, Safety Pin Girl took a swing at the Poetess, narrowly missing the ruby stud in her nose. The Poetess dropped all pretense of literary diffidence and slapped Safety in the face. Safety jumped to her feet, knocking her chair over, and dove on top of the poor Poetess, who didn't have as much practice brawling as your typical punk girl gets on an average weekend night. Holly, Mads, and I had to break *up the fight before it got bloody, which doesn't take long when you're dealing with the heavily pierced. A few of the boys sprang to our aid. Not Bowie, though; perhaps he was afraid of smudging his lightning bolt. Safety and the Poetess were ejected, and the party proceeded. I later learned that the Poetess managed a glimpse of Bowie's e-mail address and has been in touch with him. No news of an actual date yet. Maybe he's too busy making contact with his home planet.*

I suggest that from now own we should hold Speed Dating parties for different segments of the high school population. What's next—jocks and jockettes? Sk8ter Boyz and the chicks who love them? Hip-hop princes and princesses? The possibilities are endless.

"Oh, Lina!" Autumn chased after Lina on the way to biology class. They were dissecting frogs that day. "Do you have a frog partner yet?"

Lina kept walking. "Nice try, Autumn, but you can forget it. I'm stonewalling you. I'm not telling you anything, and we're not going to be lab partners. I'm not saying another word to you, starting NOW."

Autumn was now in front of her, walking backward so she could face Lina, and in danger of tripping with every step. She pouted and tried to look pitiful and helpless.

"Don't give me that look," Lina said. "I can't believe

you wrote about Pete and Tess on your blog. You stole my secrets! I was an idiot to trust you."

"I'm not trying to get your secrets," Autumn said. "I just want to be your lab partner."

"Please."

"Come on, Lina. What are you so mad about? Walker is still talking to me. In fact, this morning he told me all about how wild you and he got last night—"

"Liar! I didn't see him last night." Lina remembered her vow not to speak to Autumn at all. She was doing a lousy job of it. "And I'm not talking to you anymore. Starting NOW!"

"But you'll still be my lab partner, right?" Autumn said.

Lina shook her head.

"You can't keep this up forever," Autumn said.

Lina made a zipping motion across her mouth and stalked into the biology room. She went up to the first person she saw and said, "Be my lab partner?"

"Uh, okay," Ramona said.

"Lina's *my* lab partner," Autumn said.

"I am not," Lina said to Ramona. "Tell her I'm not. She only wants to be my lab partner so she can find out secrets about me to post on her Web of lies."

"Give it up, Autumn," Ramona said. "Her secrets are mine now. You lose."

"That's what I get for trying to be friendly," Autumn huffed.

"Yeah, right," Lina said. "Friendly. She's trying to beat me to that internship. By stealing my stories! She's got nerve. How dumb does she think I am?"

"You did fall for it the first time," Ramona said. "She probably thought it was worth another shot." She paused. Lina braced herself for what was coming next. "I *do* read your column, you know."

"You don't mind what I wrote about you, do you?" Lina asked. "It wasn't exactly a secret, the fight and everything. There were dozens of witnesses."

"You could have checked your facts with me first," Ramona said. "I wasn't hot for the David Bowie guy. I just didn't want to waste six minutes talking to Yucky Gilbert." The boy in the cape. "Even if I was willing to stoop that low, which I'm not, everyone knows Mads is his true love. He only signed up for the party because he knew she'd be there without her boyfriend."

This was all true. Much to Mads' horror, Yucky Gilbert, a cape-wearing, twelve-year-old freshman geek, had declared his love for her earlier that year. It was also true that even Ramona, with her unusual tastes, would never want to go out with him.

"I would have thought you'd *like* the cape," Lina said.

"On some people, maybe. On Bowie, sure. But on a boy who dresses as R2-D2, Halloween or not, no."

"How's your internship application going, by the way?" Lina asked.

"I submitted some poems," Ramona said. "But that bitch Erica said she doesn't like poetry. Can you believe that? Doesn't like poetry! I'm surprised she's willing to admit it."

"Well, it's true that most newspapers don't publish much poetry," Lina said.

"They used to," Ramona said. "And they should. Anyway, I need to find a new approach. Maybe I'll write some more journalistic-type articles for her, stuff like the spiritual malaise gripping RSAGE students, or how popular people have no souls. I think I can prove that popularity actually sucks your soul out of you. Take Rebecca. Remember her back in like sixth grade, when she was tubby and had braces and she used to be kind of sweet? Now look at her. Vapid monster."

"Well, if I can't win the internship, I hope you get it," Lina said. "Anyone but Autumn. I'm really mad at her."

"Thanks for your support. Now that you've gotten rid of her, are we really going to be lab partners?"

Lina glanced around the classroom. Everyone else had already paired up. There was no one left but her and Ramona.

"Looks that way," Lina said. "Start slicing. You can show me which of the frog's internal organs you use in your love potions."

"All my potions are vegan-friendly," Ramona said. "That eye-of-newt stuff is just a stereotype."

Nuclear Autumn: Keeping You Informed of the Latest Developments in the Life of Autumn Nelson

Pete and Tess scoop! Trouble in Paradise—Pete and Tess are on the outs! Here's the deal: Last night Tess called Pete, desperate for some nookie. If she doesn't get it every three days, she goes crazy. So he picked her up and they drove all over town looking for privacy. Tess was completely losing it. Finally Pete just pulled over on the side of the road and they started going at it right there in the car. How do I know? They were parked on Rutgers Street. I happened to drive by and saw them through the window when I was stopped at a light. They're so brazen! Tess is such a slut!

After hours of X-rated cavorting, Pete drove Tess home. This morning, he got into the car with his mother, who was driving him to school. That's when he spotted them: Tess's pink panties, right there on the floor! She forgot them in her passion the night before. Those two just can't keep track of their underwear! Pete quickly scooped them up to hide them from his mother. But where could he hide them? They'd make too much of a bulge in his pocket. So he stuffed them in his lunch bag and forgot all about them—until lunchtime today, when he opened up his bag and pulled out Tess's panties, right in front of the entire boys' swim team. The boys were passing them around and Pete lost track of them and now he doesn't know who has them. Tess heard about it, of course, and is on the rampage! Stay tuned!

On a more serious note, is anybody reading Mood Swing anymore? I mean, who cares? A bunch of freaks acting like freaks—big surprise. That blog has gone way downhill, if you ask me. If you want real dirt—dirty dirt—Nuclear Autumn is your source!

"Hey, Lina—I've got your panties!"

Lina kept her eyes forward and tried to ignore the jokes. "I could barely make it to my locker this morning," she complained to Holly and Mads outside homeroom the next day. "Stupid Autumn! Why does everybody believe her lies?"

"Because they want to?" Mads said.

"She's right about one thing: Walker is furious with me," Lina said. "I told him I had nothing to do with this. But he hates to be teased. He's afraid to be seen with me until this blows over."

"It never will, as long as Autumn gets attention for it," Holly said.

"There she is." Lina spotted Autumn walking toward them down the hall. "I'm going to have a little talk with her."

"Go get her," Mads said.

Autumn tried to hurry past Lina, but Lina matched her step for step. "Say it: You made that whole story up. I know you did, and you know you did. But I want to hear you say it."

"I don't know what you're talking about," Autumn said. "I didn't write anything about you. I wrote about Peter and Tess. And everything I wrote about Peter and Tess is true."

"But there is no Peter and Tess," Lina said.

"They're pseudonyms," Autumn said.

"I know that," Lina said. "They're pseudonyms for me and Walker. And everybody knows it."

"Well, I'm using those names to talk about a different couple," Autumn said.

"What different couple? Everyone thinks you're writing about me!" Lina could barely contain her fury.

"That's not my fault," Autumn said. "It's your own fault."

"Just stop using those names," Lina said.

"I can use any names I want to. And I have the right to put whatever I want on my blog. So what if I did make it up? I'm allowed. And if everyone believes it, that just proves I'm a good writer. That's what Erica Howard told me. She loves Nuclear Autumn now. She said she's addicted."

"She must have an addictive personality," Lina said. "She gets addicted to blogs pretty easily."

"Whatev."

"So you're not going to stop?" Lina said.

"Are you kidding? My hits are through the roof."

"Not even if it's the right thing to do?"

Autumn rolled her eyes. "The right thing for you, maybe. The right thing for me is to have the hottest blog in school and to win that internship. Bye!"

She disappeared into a classroom and shut the door behind her. The bell rang. It was time for class.

I'm not going to lose the internship to Autumn this way, Lina vowed. *And I won't let her spread lies about me and ruin my life. There has to be a way to stop her. All I have to do is find a weak point. And Autumn has plenty of those.*

12 By the Light of the Neon Milk Shake

To:	hollygolitely
From:	your daily horoscope

HERE IS TODAY'S HOROSCOPE: CAPRICORN: Your ideal love involves chocolates and a pounding heartbeat, so be sure to keep a defibrillator on hand at all times.

I don't know what it is about him," Holly said to Sebastiano one afternoon at Vineland. She was recounting her date with Eli, trying to understand why she'd enjoyed it so much. Maybe talking it out would help.

"I think I know what it is," Sebastiano said. "Could it be those big, anime eyes? Or that wiry but strong build? I know some girls really lose it over that type. Or the whole sensitive, mysterious enigma trip?"

"I guess," Holly said. "It's the way he holds back. He doesn't seem out of control the way most boys do. I probably shouldn't like him so much. He seems like he's hiding something, and his family sounds completely bonkers. You know his mother's maid tried to stab her with her own diamond-covered stiletto heel? So now she's hooked on painkillers."

"What kind? Can he get you some?"

"Stop it."

Sebastiano laughed. "He told you that? That can't be true."

"Why not? Weird things happen all the time."

"Yeah, but that's too crazy," Sebastiano said. "It does sound kind of familiar, though. Where could I have heard that story before?"

"On the news, maybe?" Holly said. She herself didn't remember any news stories like that, but she didn't always follow the news. And it probably happened a long time ago. "Or in the paper?"

"Maybe," Sebastiano said. "But I don't think so. You know, when you first told me about that whole '3:17' bit, I thought I'd heard it before, too."

"You just like to think you know everything," Holly said.

"I *do* know everything."

"But you don't know where you heard all this stuff before," Holly said.

"I know it," Sebastiano said. "It's buried somewhere in my memory. It will pop up eventually."

"I'm sure it will."

"You could do a little snooping around," Sebastiano said. "You might dig up something that would jog my memory."

"I don't want to spy on him again," Holly said.

"You said yourself you think he's hiding something."

"I know, but I felt weird about that last time," Holly said. "If he's going to be my soul mate, I should trust him, shouldn't I?"

"That sounds like something somebody would say. So when are you seeing him again?"

"Tonight," Holly said.

"Ooh, the school night date. Very risqué."

"I did most of my homework in study hall today. We're going to see a play. *Scream: The Musical*."

"Sounds icky. Have fun. I'll let you know if I remember anything juicy."

"Sorry about the play," Eli said. They sat in his car outside the Carlton Bay Playhouse. *Scream: The Musical* had been much more screaming than musical.

"That's okay," Holly said. "I kind of knew what to expect. I saw the last play they put on here. My friend Mads was in it. Her mother wrote it."

"Was it good?"

Holly didn't want to badmouth Mads or her mother, but Mads herself would have said the play sucked. Holly saw a middle ground and lunged for it. "Let's just say it was good preparation for tonight. It didn't have the blood and gore, and yet, there were casualties."

Eli put his key in the ignition. "So what do you want to do now? Are you hungry?"

"Let's hit Harvey's Carry-out and get some fries," Holly said.

"Good idea. We can sit at a picnic table and eat by the glow of the big neon milk shake." Harvey's was covered with neon, and its logo was a giant yellow milk shake cup with a peppermint-striped straw.

Eli tossed his wallet on the dashboard and started the car. Holly reached for the wallet.

"What are you doing?" Eli asked.

"I just wanted to look at your driver's license," Holly said.

Eli snatched the wallet away and stuffed it in his jacket pocket. "You can't just open up somebody's wallet like that. Anyway, it's a terrible picture. I'd hate for it to get lodged in your mind. I look like a monkey."

"I'm sorry." They were quiet for the rest of the ride to Harvey's. Holly's cheeks burned with embarrassment. She felt as if she'd just been yelled at by a teacher. On the other hand, how terrible could his picture be? She tried to imagine his face merged with a monkey's. It came out looking like Chim Chim, the pet monkey on *Speed Racer*. Maybe Sebastiano had a point about that anime thing.

They pulled up at Harvey's and got out. They ordered fries and shakes and sat on a picnic table to wait for their order to be ready. An SUV full of kids pulled up. Holly noticed a Griffith Academy sticker on the back windshield.

Four guys and a girl piled out of the SUV. "Eli!" one boy said. "What you up to tonight, dude?"

"Just marinating," Eli said. "This is Holly. Holly, this is Wes, Jake, Little Jake, Jesse, and Val."

"Hi," Holly said. The Griffith kids said hi and stared at her curiously. *This is good,* Holly thought. *A chance to meet his friends and find out a little more about him. He can't be much of a mystery to the kids he goes to school with every day.*

"We just came from the new *Force Field* flick," Wes said. "It rocked."

"Don't listen to him," Val said. "It was so stupid."

"Order up!" the girl called from the pickup window.

Eli jumped up. "That's our stuff." He went to the window to get the food, then carried it to his car. "I'll see you guys tomorrow."

"Wait," Wes said. "We'll order and you can hang with us. We're going to hit the Roadhouse and see if anybody good's playing."

"That sounds like fun," Holly said.

"We can't, though," Eli said. "Holly's got a curfew. Very strict parents. School night and everything." He opened the passenger door for Holly and gestured for her to get in. She did, taking the food on her lap. He hurried to the driver's side, got in, and started the car.

"Nice to meet you, Holly," Val said.

Eli waved to his friends and pulled out.

"I thought we were going to eat by the glow of the neon milk shake," Holly said.

"The place was crawling with mosquitoes," Eli said. "You didn't feel them?"

"No," Holly said. "It's a little early in the year for mosquitoes." *There weren't any mosquitoes*, Holly thought. *It was his friends. Does he not want me to talk to them for some reason? Is he ashamed of me? Or of them?*

Or was he afraid they'd reveal something to her—something he didn't want her to know? Like maybe another girl? That could be it: He had a girlfriend at Griffith, and

123

he was cheating on her with Holly! Or cheating on Holly with her! She had no proof, but it was the most logical explanation.

He pulled off at the same scenic overlook they'd stopped at before. It was beautiful, the clouds blowing across the sky, brushing past the moon. They nibbled French fries and sucked on their shakes.

"I didn't mean to run away like that," Eli said at last. "It's just . . . my friends can be such jerks. I wanted a romantic night with you, and it would be impossible with them around, shooting spitballs at us or whatever."

Holly wanted to get to know his friends, because she was curious about him. But when he explained it this way, she understood.

"The moon's nicer than a neon milk shake, anyway," she said.

Eli set his drink aside and took her face in both hands. She was caught putting a fry into her mouth. It was now stuck in limbo between her teeth. Eli bit off the end.

"Holly," he whispered. "Do you know what you've done to me?"

"What I've done to you?" Holly asked.

"To my heart," Eli said. "And my head. And my soul."

Oh. "I wasn't trying to hurt them, if that's what you mean," Holly said.

"You haven't hurt them, not yet. And I hope you never will. But you've made them grow. You've made them sing. My heart beats like a mariachi, pumping its rhythms all through the rest of me. I'm hooked on you, Holly. I need you the way diabetics need injections of insulin. If I can't see you, I can't live. My life is in your hands."

Holly's French fry sat chewed in her mouth, unswallowed. She couldn't move her throat. She was surprised by his words. She let them sink in, and they acted like sugar, boosting her energy and making her glow.

"Don't worry, you can see me," she said. "I'm happy to see you anytime."

She quickly swallowed, afraid he was going to kiss her. She didn't want him to get a mouthful of potato.

Still holding her face in his hands, he gently kissed her. She closed her eyes. She could feel the moonlight on her face as if it had heat like the sun. But she knew it didn't. The heat must have come from some other source.

He lifted his lips off of hers and pressed them to her forehead. Then he held her close. He smelled like cinnamon and cloves. It made her think of her grandfather's pipe tobacco. He smelled so good, she nuzzled her face in his neck. They held each other this way for a long time. When he dropped her off at home an hour later, he gave her that one sweet kiss again, and said good night.

• • •

"No, I'm sorry," Mads said. "I've got to know more. Something's weird about this guy. You've got to find out what he's hiding."

Holly had invited Mads and Lina over for lunch on Saturday afternoon. They were rehashing Holly's last Eli date. Mads and Lina were both stuck on the mysterious parts, like why he wouldn't let her look inside his wallet, and why he was so anxious to get away from his friends. For Holly, those things lingered in the back of her mind, but the kissing, and his smell, stayed up front.

"Why don't we go drive by his house?" Lina said. "Just to see what it looks like. You haven't seen it yet, have you?"

"No," Holly said.

"Aren't you curious?"

"I am," Mads said. "Maybe we could get a look at his mother's stiletto wounds. So gruesome, yet glamorous."

"I don't know where he lives," Holly said.

"We'll look him up in the phone book." Lina took the phone book from the top of the refrigerator and started flipping through it. "His last name is Collins?"

Holly nodded. "But look, there are four other Collinses in town. And his family's rich. They're probably unlisted."

Mads pointed to a listing for Collins, Eli, 620 Blue Hill Road. "Maybe that's Eli, Sr. Is Eli a junior?"

"I don't know," Holly said. "I guess he could be. And Blue Hill Road isn't far from Griffith."

"We'll drive by," Lina said. "If you see his car in the driveway, you'll know it's the right house."

"Come on, let's do it," Mads said. "You went spying with Sebastiano last week. It's our turn now."

"Okay, why not," Holly said. "But if he's outside and sees us, I'm going to duck."

"But you'll be driving," Lina said.

"Spying is dangerous work," Holly said.

"We'll take our chances," Mads said.

They drove downtown. Turning north and away from the bay, they found Blue Hill Road. The first houses were large old Victorians, built when the town was founded. As they drove away from the center of town the street became more modern, with split levels and ranch houses from the 1940s, '50s, and '60s, fewer trees, more lawn.

"There it is," Mads said. "620 Blue Hill."

It was a 50s ranch house, very ordinary-looking. A blue Honda was parked in the driveway. Also a new Buick. "That Honda is his car," Holly said. "But that can't be his house."

"Why not?" Lina asked.

How to explain? It just didn't look right to Holly. It wasn't the way she'd pictured his house at all. It wasn't the kind of house where maids stabbed people with diamond stilettos. Or even the kind of house where people *owned* diamond stilettos. Or any kind of stilettos. It was just a regular old suburban house.

"Someone's coming out," Mads said.

The front door opened, and two middle-aged people emerged. They walked toward the Buick. The woman looked fit, with a sensible, short haircut, brown tinged with gray. She wore a green sweatsuit and sneakers. The man had a slight paunch, was balding, and wore slacks and a windbreaker. They got into the Buick and pulled out. Holly ducked.

"Is that the painkiller addict?" Mads asked.

"She doesn't look like the type to wear diamond-covered shoes," Lina said. "And she wasn't in a wheelchair."

"And I thought his father lived on a ranch in Santa Barbara," Mads said. "Not a ranch *house*."

"Maybe that was his stepfather," Holly said, though Eli hadn't mentioned a stepfather.

"A stepfather named Eli Collins, Sr.?" Lina said. "That would be weird."

When the Buick was out of sight, Holly pulled into the driveway. A small sign hung from a lamppost on the walk leading to the house. Holly wanted to get closer so she could read it.

"ELI COLLINS, DDS," it said, with an arrow pointing toward a side door where an office must be.

"He's a dentist?" Holly said. "Eli's father is a dentist?"

"I guess you could be a rancher *and* a dentist," Mads said, surveying the half-acre yard.

"Something weird is going on," Holly said. "Eli is lying to me."

13 The News from Lake Hobegone

To:	mad4u
From:	your daily horoscope

HERE IS TODAY'S HOROSCOPE: VIRGO: You think you've got problems? Try eating tainted sushi. Then you'll really know problems.

Does Ginny actually know anything about modern dance?" Quintana asked. "I've taken a lot of dance classes, but never one where the teacher uses a whistle."

Mads laughed. "I know. She's like, *'Tweet!* Point those toes! *Tweet!* Be one with the floor! *Tweet tweet!* You are a wind-blown cloud!'"

Gym Group 3 was in the locker room changing after

class. The sophomores were divided into four gym sections, which changed every quarter. Group 3 had modern dance with Ginny the Gym Teacher. This quarter, Mads was in a different section from Holly and Lina, who were still out on the track, running hurdles and learning to high jump.

"Ginny's always taught dance that way," Ingrid said. "I don't see anything weird about it."

"You don't?" Quintana said. "I don't know, that whistle . . . it's so . . . gym-teacher-esque."

"That's why they call it gym," Ingrid said.

"What-evah," Quintana said. She stretched her arms over her head, then swooped down and pressed her head to her knees, holding her ankles. Her body was lean and strong, made for a leotard. Mads, who'd taken her share of dance classes, had always envied that type: the natural dancer's body.

"What-evah," Ingrid sneered. "Is that how they talk in Lake Ho-begone, or wherever it is you moved here from?"

"You mean, Los Angeles?" Quintana said.

"Same thing, from what I hear," Ingrid said. "Slutsville."

"I knew Carlton Bay was a small town when we moved here," Quintana said, "but I had no idea that people who live so close to San Francisco could be so provincial."

"Shows what you know," Ingrid said.

Mads quietly took off her sweaty leotard, listening to

the conversation. Ingrid sounded silly, picking on Quintana this way. Mads couldn't help admiring Quintana's cool, which only infuriated Ingrid more. Was that the same quality the boys liked so much? Mads wasn't sure. Quintana's secret was a mystery Mads was determined to solve. And she was about to find a new clue.

Quintana peeled off her leotard like a lizard shedding its skin. Underneath she was wearing a lacy red bra and matching thong. Mads tried not to stare. But she was amazed. Her underwear was so pretty. And sexy. And grown up. Mads glanced down at her white lycra sports bra, which she barely needed, and her white cotton panties. Spanky Pants. She'd worn the same brand since she was in third grade.

All around her, the other girls were wearing white cotton like Mads, or bikinis and boy shorts and bras in cute colors and patterns. Kid stuff. No one was wearing anything lacy and silky and see-through. Except Quintana.

"You can always tell a Slutsville girl by her underwear," Ingrid stage-whispered to Claire. Quintana ignored them. Mads tried to shut them out.

"You wear thongs?" she asked Quintana. "And lacy pushup bras?"

"Of course," Quintana said. "I'd die before I'd wear granny pants. They might go in and out of fashion, but who wants to feel like a grandma? Silk feels so sexy, even if no one ever sees it. And when you feel sexy, you act sexy." She reached for her blouse, and the silk shimmered against her skin.

How did Quintana know all this? Mads had to admit that standing next to Quintana, thong to granny pants, she felt like a tomboy. Or a little kid. And Quintana looked like a woman. Or a lingerie ad.

Maybe that's the secret, Mads thought. *If I wear sexy lingerie when I'm with Stephen, I'll feel sexy. He'll pick up on the vibe and feel sexy, too. And then maybe we can make out for five minutes without some kind of lame interruption.*

"The key is, everything has to fit right," Quintana said to Mads. "Especially bras. Actually, I need some new stuff. Want to go to Victoria's Secret with me this afternoon?"

"Sure!" Mads said. This was an opportunity Mads wouldn't miss for anything. Lingerie shopping with the sleek Quintana. Who knew what tips she'd pick up?

"That will be a sight," Ingrid said. "Little Mads all dolled up in a lacy bra. She doesn't even have enough to fill an A cup."

"I'd rather be too small on top than too big on the bottom," Quintana said with a glance at Ingrid's too-tiny panties.

"Bite me," Ingrid snapped.

"And risk salmonella poisoning?" Quintana said. "No thanks."

"Try this camisole," Quintana said, holding up a sheer top made of fine, pale-pink netting. It was simple but pretty. "The good thing about being an A-cup is you can wear things like this and you don't need a bra." She stretched the fabric over her hand. Her tawny skin glowed through it.

Mads tried on the camisole, and it looked beautiful on her. On her paler skin, the pink made her look rosy. It was comfortable, too. She added it to the pile of things she'd decided to buy: a lacy bra in hot purple ("This will look great under a tank with your straps showing," Quintana told her), a pair of sheer black panties, and a tiny striped thong, practically a string. It was the one item Mads wasn't too sure about, comfort-wise. But she felt she should have one. And Quintana said it looked evil on her, which was a good thing.

"Thanks for coming with me," Quintana said as they paid for their things. She had bought a pair of satin tap pants with a matching cami. "It really helps to have a friend with you when you're buying lingerie."

"I know," Mads said. "I could never have done this alone." Which was way beyond true. If Quintana hadn't urged her on, she would have run screaming back to the granny pants section.

"You're so cute," Quintana said. "You just need to believe it." She stood next to a giant poster showing a line of Victoria's Secret models, and Mads was struck by how much Quintana fit in with them. Quintana was not as voluptuous as the models, but they shared a kind of ripe look. And an uninhibited quality. That was what the boys liked, for sure. The question was, did you have to be born with it? Or could you manufacture it somehow? Mads was hoping it would rub off of Quintana and onto her, because she wasn't born with it, that was for sure.

QUIZ: WHAT IS YOUR UNDERWEAR PERSONALITY?

What does your underwear say about you? Probably more than you realize. Take this quiz and find out your lingerie type.

1. **Your favorite kind of panties are:**
    & ❏ granny pants
    # ❏ boy shorts
    *, # ❏ bikinis
    % ❏ thong
    *, %❏ none

2. **You'd wear a thong even though it's uncomfortable:**
    $, %❏ True
    *,& ❏ False

3. **Your favorite bra type is:**

   \#   ❏ sports bra

   &   ❏ heavy duty cotton holster in plain white

   \$ ❏ lacy, flimsy

   %   ❏ pushup bra

   *   ❏ none

4. **Extras: Choose your favorite:**

   \$ ❏ thigh-high stockings

   %   ❏ corset

   &   ❏ lacy camisole

   %   ❏ garter belt

   &   ❏ tummy-control body shaper

   &   ❏ day-of-the-week panties

   *   ❏ panties with a sexy message on them

   \#   ❏ plain white tank undershirt

   \$ ❏ teddy

   &   ❏ tap pants

5. **The most important quality your underwear should have is:**

   \#   ❏ comfort

   %   ❏ sex appeal

   \$ ❏ style, fashionability

   *   ❏ color

   &   ❏ good, flattering fit

6. **The movie heroine you most identify with is:**

*, $ ❏ Julia Roberts in *Erin Brockovich*

& ❏ Nicole Kidman in *Bewitched*

\# ❏ Lindsay Lohan in *Herbie: Fully Loaded*

$, * ❏ Lindsay Lohan in *Mean Girls*

& ❏ Julia Stiles in *Mona Lisa Smile*

% ❏ Jessica Simpson in *The Dukes of Hazard*

\# ❏ Hilary Swank in *Million Dollar Baby*

$ ❏ Angelina Jolie in *Lara Croft: Tomb Raider*

*, \# ❏ Hilary Duff in *The Lizzie McGuire Movie*

& ❏ Renée Zellweger in *Bridget Jones's Diary*

Add up how many times you checked each symbol. Whichever symbol has the most checks, that's your Underwear Personality.

*___ &___ %___ #___ $___

* Free Spirit: You like to look natural, be comfortable, and be yourself. You like to have fun without worrying about how you look—and that makes you extra fun to be around. You're effortlessly sexy.

& Prim and Proper: You are modest and don't like to have too much showing. You have an intellectual bent and would prefer to be admired for your mind and personality rather than your figure, no matter how smashing. You believe that keeping it under wraps only makes things hotter later, when the wrappings come off.

% **Bombshell:** You've got it and you like to flaunt it. You also may be curvy and can use the extra support that good lingerie gives. You're sexy and flirtatious and always up for a good time.

Sporty Girl: You're athletic and like your underwear to be practical, functional, and comfortable because you are on the go. You believe a body in motion is sexier than one trussed up in a lot of frills.

$ **Adventuress:** You like high-style, edgy fashion, and the underwear that goes with it. You're bold and daring and only interested in people with the energy to keep up with you.

14 Never Fear, Ramona's Here

To:	linaonme
From:	your daily horoscope

HERE IS TODAY'S HOROSCOPE: CANCER: If your conscience is bothering you, just bonk yourself on the head. That should take care of it.

Nuclear Autumn: Keeping You Informed of the Latest Developments in the Lives of Autumn Nelson, Peter, and Tess

Forget about me for the moment (I never thought I'd say that!)—my life is a complete bore compared with the passion that is Pete and Tess. To the casual observer, Tess seems calm, even sensible. Little do you all know! Yesterday I caught her under the bleachers at the lacrosse field. The boys' lacrosse team was practicing, but Tess wasn't watching them. She was facing the other way, watching the gym parking lot through binoculars—and swigging vodka out of a bottle! "Tess," I said. "What are you doing? If someone catches you drinking on campus, you could get expelled!"

"I don't give a ——" she said. (I won't print what she said, because I don't condone vulgarity on my blog.) "Peter is cheating on me. Look!"

She passed the binoculars to me. She looked terrible and reeked of vodka. I peered through the binocs and saw Pete in a car with a blonde. "Oh, my god," I said, "is that——?"

"——my best friend," Tess said. "Or rather, one of my two best friends. The blonde, slutty one. Not the dark-haired, pudgy one. The one who doesn't have a boyfriend in spite of the fact that she's so fast. Which only goes to show boys don't really like sluts, in the end."

I looked again. Pete was definitely playing doctor with Tess's best friend, Polly (not her real name). No wonder Tess was hitting the bottle. She started to cry. I put my arm around her, trying to comfort her in spite of her terrible smell. "Poor Tess," I said. "It must be awful knowing you can't keep a boy interested in you for more than a few weeks."

"I know," she said. "I'm such a loser." But then her tears suddenly turned to rage. "I won't stand for this," she seethed. "I'm

going to get my revenge on Polly. She won't know what hit her.
I'll pretend I don't know what's going on behind my back. But
when she least expects it—wham!"

Polly, if you're reading this—and you know who you
are—this is a warning to you: Watch your back. I'd hate to see
anyone get hurt. (I think Tess might know tae bo.)

"Okay, I know this is ridiculous, but I just want to
make 100 percent sure you know I'm not fooling around
with Walker," Holly said. She sat next to Lina and Mads
at their usual lunch table.

"I know," Lina said. "You're not the problem. It's everyone else in school. Nobody even calls me Lina anymore.
They call me Tess and snicker behind my back."

"What about me?" Holly said. "Polly—that's not even
an attempt to hide my identity. And she totally defamed
me. She called me a slut who's fooling around with her
best friend's boyfriend. And I would never do that."

"It's crazy. How can anyone possibly believe
Autumn's stories?" Lina said.

"The line between truth and fiction has been blurred,"
Holly said.

"I heard Rebecca say that if the first Pete and Tess
stories were true, why not these?" Mads said.

"The major difference is, I wrote the first stories and

Autumn is writing the new ones." Lina was paralyzed with frustration and anger. "I mean, smell me. Smell me! Have I ever, as long as you've known me, reeked of vodka? I've never drunk vodka, not once in my whole life."

Mads put an arm around her. "No, you've never smelled like vodka. Don't worry. No one could possibly believe that. You always smell like a mix of lavender shampoo and pencil shavings."

"It's a very sweet smell," Holly added.

"Tess. Polly. Mads." Ramona sat down at their table in the lunchroom. "You're the only one without a Nuclear Autumn nickname, Mads."

"I feel so left out," Mads said.

"I'm sure she'll get around to you," Lina said.

"You can't let her get away with this," Ramona said. "The whole school is lapping it up. The wilder her stories get, the more people want to believe them."

"I'll write a Mood Swing rebuttal," Lina said.

"That will never work," Ramona said. "You've got to fight fire with fire. Start a bunch of rumors about Autumn, so she has to go on the defensive. Then she won't have so much time to attack you."

"I can't do that," Lina said. "I don't have any dirt on her."

"Duh. Make it up," Ramona said.

"But that's . . . that's not right," Lina said.

"Who cares?" Ramona said.

"What Autumn is doing isn't right, either," Mads said.

"No," Lina said. "I can't." It was tempting—so tempting—to trash Autumn in her blog. But she was a high-road kind of girl. And, anyway, if she stuck to her journalistic principles, she'd have a better shot at the internship. "I'm not Autumn. I'd rather handle this my own way. RSAGE students are smart. I'm sure if I appeal to their sense of decency and truth, I will prevail."

Mads suppressed a snicker.

"It's your funeral," Ramona said.

"And our reputations," Holly said.

Mood Swing
Current Mood: Concerned
To all Nuclear Autumn readers:

Autumn has been writing about some people who supposedly go to RSAGE: Peter, Tess, and now Polly. I can't say for sure that she is making these stories up out of nothing, though I suspect she is. But one thing I do know for sure: The exploits of Peter and Tess have nothing to do with me or my life. There is not one grain of truth in any of those stories. Okay, yes, I have a boyfriend, and I have a friend whose name rhymes with Polly, but that's as far as it goes. Walker is not cheating on me with "Polly" or anyone else. I didn't leave my panties in his car. I don't drink vodka or own a pair of binoculars.

I know it's fun to read these stories. But, please, I beg everyone to understand that they are just that—stories. Let's all calm down and stop this speeding gossip train before it runs off the tracks!

Nuclear Autumn: Keeping You Informed of the Latest Developments in the Lives of Autumn Nelson, Peter, and Tess

I know nobody reads Mood Swing anymore, so if you missed it (totally understandable), here's an update: Lina is accusing me of making up my gossip! Don't listen to her! Everything I write is true. She's just trying to spin things her way. Damage control. Like Congressmen do when they get caught with their pants down. My readers are too smart to fall for that. So ignore Mood Swing and keep your dial tuned right here! More Pete and Tess news on the way. Tess was last seen coming on to a junior of the male persuasion, in a desperate attempt to make Pete jealous. The junior didn't look too interested. Good luck, honey!

"Satisfied?" Ramona asked. She and Lina were in biology lab. Ramona was poking through their dead frog in search of its heart. Lina could hardly bear to look at it, lying there pinned to the mat with its stomach sliced open and its insides exposed.

"I give up," Lina said. "She's evil. Unstoppable. No one will listen to me. No one wants to hear the truth. And Autumn's being rewarded for lying!" She hung her head, nose away from the frog because of the formaldehyde smell. "What can I do? It's hopeless! Autumn is free to ruin my life as she pleases."

"You need help," Ramona said. "Supernatural help. Never fear. Ramona's here."

"How can *you* help me?"

"Your big weakness: scruples," Ramona said. "When dealing with a girl like Autumn, scruples are a handicap. I'll steer you away from your scrupulous impulses and show you the path to the dark side. I've always thought your dark side was a lot closer to the surface than you were willing to admit, anyway. Welcome to the nether regions of the soul."

Lina didn't say so, but she knew Ramona was right. "All right. Dark side, here I come."

15 Los Días del Corazón

HERE IS TODAY'S HOROSCOPE: CAPRICORN: Your life has become a romantic cliché so stale, even the cast members of *Friends* refuse to play you in the movie.

I t's like he's leading a double life," Holly said. "Everything Eli told me about his family seems to be a lie."

She and Sebastiano sat side-by-side in the school hallway, leaning against their lockers. Kids stepped over their outstretched legs as they walked by. Holly was telling Sebastiano about Eli's parents and their dentist's office-slash-house.

"But why would he lie?" Holly said. "His parents looked perfectly normal."

"Maybe they're *too* normal," Sebastiano said. "Maybe he's trying to impress you by pretending to be glamorous."

"But if he has any intention of being my boyfriend, I'm sure to find out the truth eventually, and then what?" She sighed. "He's not serious about me."

"Could he be insane?" Sebastiano asked. "Have you considered mental illness?"

"He's not insane," Holly said. "But he is confusing. Or else he's a con man. The last time I saw him, we had a great time. I didn't mention that I'd looked up his address and spied on him at his house and found out everything he'd told me to that point was a lie, so he kept them coming. He said his father was married three times before he met his mother, which is why his sibling situation is too complicated to explain. But one of his half brothers is an oil magnate, and his favorite half sister is in prison for embezzlement on trumped-up charges. Seems she was framed by one of her stepmothers—I forget which one."

"This all sounds so familiar," Sebastiano said.

"You keep saying that," Holly said. "Could it describe *your* family?"

"Almost, but that's not it. The more you tell me the more it nags at me. . . ."

"What I don't understand is how, after telling me all that—which I guess is all lies, but who knows?—how can he turn to me, kiss me, and say, 'The sky meets the water in your eyes.'"

"That's it!" Sebastiano smacked his forehead dramatically. "I've heard that line before. All these details you've told me about Eli—I know them from somewhere. And I finally figured out where."

"Where?"

"*Los Días del Corazón!*"

"What?"

"*Days of the Heart*. It's a Mexican 'telenovela'. A soap opera. Totally wild, very juicy. Those Mexicans know how to do daytime drama."

"What are you talking about?"

"It's on one of those Spanish cable channels," Sebastiano said. "My babysitter used to watch the telenovelas when I was little. She got me hooked. I still tune in every once in a while."

Holly was shocked. "What are you saying? Everything Eli has said to me since I met him comes from a Mexican soap opera? How can that be?"

"It's true—even that '3:17' thing. The very first words he said to you. Otavio used that line on Marisol just a few weeks ago. I knew I'd heard it somewhere before."

"Otavio?"

"You'd love him—he's gorgeous. He's the heartthrob of the show, but a real cad. Women part for him like the Red Sea for Moses."

"Ugh, Sebastiano . . ." This was all so weird.

"But Marisol is the only one who can stand up to him. His equal. She's beautiful, sexy, unattainable . . . until Otavio used that line about always thinking of her at that moment in time. Only on the show, I think the time was 11:42."

Holly was steaming mad. Her entire relationship with Eli—what there was of it—was a complete fiction? Based on a TV show? How could he be so brazen?

"After that, Marisol is smitten, but she doesn't show it," Sebastiano said. "She waits for him to call—but Otavio doesn't call for a long time. He wants to make her want him, really want him. But he's also kind of busy defending the ranch against a raid by some evil drug lords who are blackmailing his father."

"At least Eli didn't try to get me to believe that," Holly said, thinking of Eli, Sr., the paunchy dentist. "But Eli did make me wait before he called me—and he had some kind of crazy excuse. It's as if he's following the show like a script. The little bugger. What happened next?"

"Well, I missed the episode where the maid stabs the

mother with the diamond stiletto heel, but I saw the maid burying the bloody shoe in the garden. Otavio and Marisol have a romantic dinner, but Otavio takes it slowly. He's usually the Don Juan type, but with Marisol he just gives her a single, chaste kiss."

"Oh, my god." That was exactly what Eli had done with her. Only none of it was real. He was copying a character on a Mexican soap opera. And she had fallen for it. But it was all fake. Were his feelings for her fake, too?

The anger rose up in her and drove her to her feet. Eli wouldn't get away with this. "That asshole!" she cried. "I can't believe what a jerk he is!"

Sebastiano stayed seated on the floor. "It's kind of funny, if you think about it," he said. "Don't step on my hand." Holly was pacing furiously back and forth in front of the lockers.

"He's going to pay," Holly said. "I am going to go over there to his *ranch house* where he lives with his *dentist father* and tell him off like he's never been told off before. I'll let him know what I think of his Mexican soap opera. And then I'm going to dump him and never speak to him again, no matter how pathetically he begs." Assuming he would beg. Holly dearly hoped he would, so she could hang up the phone on him and let his e-mails go unanswered as the situation warranted.

She turned to Sebastiano and practically spat, "I'm leaving now. You coming? You enjoy the sight of blood, don't you?"

Sebastiano jumped up. "Wait, wait, wait a second here."

"I don't want to wait. I want to go this minute while my rage is good and hot. I'll make him look at the clock and tell me what time it is—before I dump him. Another priceless moment he'll never forget."

"Stop," Sebastiano said. "Let's think this through."

"What's there to think about?" Holly said. "I understand that Eli is a jerk. Therefore, I will break up with him. Period."

He grabbed Holly's arm and tried to calm her down. "You can do that, but then you'll miss all the fun."

"What fun? I see nothing fun about this."

"Think about it," Sebastiano said. "Don't you get it? The tables have turned. You know his secret. And he doesn't know you know."

"So?"

"So now *you* have the power," Sebastiano said. "This is a dream come true! He's following that soap opera like it's a script for his life. All you have to do is watch the show, and you can predict everything he's going to say and do. Don't you see? You can do more than just dump

151

his ass. You can totally mess with his head."

Holly's mind instantly cleared. The idea was very appealing. "It will be like being able to read his thoughts," she said. "If I watch the show, I'll know exactly what Eli's going to do next. I'll be prepared for everything."

"You'll be able to have a little fun with him," Sebastiano said. "Torture him a little. Make him pay for what he's done to you."

"Yeah." Holly's mood brightened. "I've got a great source of information here. Why waste it? Why not put it to good use?"

"Exactly."

"Thank god I take Spanish, or I'd never be able to follow the show." She'd been taking Spanish since seventh grade. She wasn't fluent, but she had a decent grasp of it.

"He won't know that you're onto him," Sebastiano said. "But you'll always know what he's up to. You'll be able to predict his every move. Holly, come to my house after school this afternoon! We'll watch the show together. You've got to let me be a part of this—you've just got to!"

"Calm down," Holly said. "All right. Let's watch the show this afternoon. I'll be TiVo'ing it every day from now on, believe me."

"Excellent," Sebastiano said. "This is so exciting.

A real, live soap opera come to life!"

Holly wasn't nearly as thrilled as Sebastiano was. But her curiosity got the best of her. *What will happen next?* she wondered. *Stay tuned for the next episode of* Holly's Increasingly Weird Life.

16 The God of Sexy Moments Has a Laugh at Mads' Expense

To:	mad4u
From:	your daily horoscope

HERE IS TODAY'S HOROSCOPE: VIRGO: Something embarrassing will happen to you today. No, even more embarrassing than usual.

L oosen up your shoulders," Mads shouted over the music. "Like this." She took Stephen by the shoulders and shook him, trying to unstiffen him. As she shook him she felt her new thong ride up on her hips. She wiggled her hips, trying to get the thong to slip back down, but that didn't work. She had no choice but to reach down and adjust it—again.

"Like this?" Stephen waggled his shoulders and pumped his legs up and down. He looked like a robot on speed.

"Kind of, but don't jerk your head. More relaxed." Mads showed him a smooth, easy, side-to-side step. She wished *she* could be more relaxed. It was Saturday night, and she and Stephen were out at the Rutgers Roadhouse, dancing to a post-punk band called Go Dog Go. The band was great, and Stephen, in spite of congenitally dorky dancing, looked good. She wore her sexy new camisole peeking out from under a white stretch button-down shirt, and her thong under her blue suede mini. The camisole was fine, but the thong was driving her crazy. It kept riding up and getting into places where she didn't want it to be. She was constantly adjusting it, which did not make her feel the least bit sexy.

"Is this better?" Stephen was pogo'ing now, a dance move even a boy couldn't mess up. Mads nodded. That song segued into another fast tune. Stephen took her hands so they could hop up and down together. She put her arms around his neck and jumped up on his back, wrapping her legs around his waist. He laughed and tried to pogo while piggybacking her.

That's when it happened.

Mads felt a tiny *ping!* on the side of her hip. A snap,

as if somebody had flicked her with a fingernail. She quickly unhooked her legs and jumped off Stephen's back. He kept pogo'ing, but she didn't. He stopped.

"What's wrong?" he asked.

Mads didn't answer at first. She could feel something hanging off her left leg. A swatch of fabric against her thigh. She reached to her right hip to tug the thong strap up. But it wasn't there.

Oh, my god.

She glanced down and spotted a thin blue string peeking out from under her skirt.

"Gotta go—bathroom emergency!" she shouted over the music. She ran to the ladies' room before Stephen could ask what the problem was. She couldn't think of a nonembarrassing answer.

She locked herself in a stall and inspected the damage. One thong strap had snapped. Her panties were hanging by the other strap—a thread—from her left leg. Completely useless.

She had two choices: 1. Try to mend the broken thong as best she could and carry on; or 2. Toss the stupid thong in the trash.

She opted for #1. She tied together the broken ends of the thong strap. The knot made a little lump under her skirt. Real sexy. She just hoped it would hold.

She returned to Stephen, who immediately grabbed her and flung her across the dance floor. Normally she was a wild dancer, but this was a touchy situation. Her hand involuntarily touched the knot at the side of her hip to make sure it was holding. She found herself checking the status of her thong every three minutes for the rest of the night. She couldn't let loose if she had to worry about things falling out from under her skirt.

Stephen playfully shook her shoulders. "Relax!" he teased, imitating her. "Don't be such a stiff boy dancer."

She smiled and shimmied, then checked her underwear again. Still holding . . . whoops. As she touched it, the knot came undone.

"Um, I have to go to the bathroom again," she said.

Stephen looked concerned. "Are you sure you're okay?" he asked.

"Yeah," she said. "But when I get back, can we leave?"

"Whatever you want."

She returned to the bathroom and tossed the useless string into the trash. Mads knew lots of ways to ruin a night out: talking too much, not talking enough, saying something stupid, bursting into tears . . . She'd been guilty of date-busters before. But rogue lingerie? This was a new one.

So much for the thong experiment—it was back to granny pants for her.

17 Tess's Tresses

HERE IS TODAY'S HOROSCOPE: CANCER: Your life feels like a horror film and you're the babysitter.

O w!" Lina felt a sharp tug on the back of her hair. She turned around. Karl Levine, a dopey guy in her Interpersonal Human Development class, laughed and ran away to the safety of his lunchroom table full of geeks. "What did you do that for?" Lina called after him.

"That was weird," Holly said.

"*Karl's* weird," Mads said. "Tell us more about the show."

They were having lunch while Holly explained the Eli situation to them. She and Sebastiano had watched the first episode of *Los Días del Corazón* the day before.

"Otavio is this hunky guy who's always taking his shirt off," Holly said.

"Does he look like Eli?" Lina asked.

"No," Holly said. "Then there's Marisol, a beautiful brunette who lives in a bikini."

"Does she look like you?" Mads asked.

"No," Holly said. "But listen to this: Yesterday Otavio sent Marisol roses with this incredible note saying how passionate he was for her. And a few hours later I got roses from Eli!"

"What did the note say?" Lina asked.

"It said, 'Thinking of you at 3:17.'"

"Wow," Mads said.

"What else happened?" Lina asked.

"Otavio threatened Marisol's ex-boyfriend," Holly said. "He said he'd kill him if he ever came near Marisol again."

"Do you think Eli will threaten Rob?" Mads lowered her voice—even though the lunchroom was so noisy, Rob wouldn't have heard her if she'd shouted. He was sitting with his swim team buddies. One of them was trying to keep a potato chip in the air as long as he could by blowing at it through a straw. Rob wore a T-shirt that said, GOT RID OF THE KIDS—THE CAT WAS ALLERGIC.

Holly shrugged. "Who knows? I hope not. Rob hasn't done anything to bother me. We haven't even spoken."

Lina felt another tweak at the back of her head. She whipped her head around. Claire Kessler stood sheepishly behind her.

"Stop it!" Lina snapped. "Why did you do that?"

"I just wanted to see if it's true," Claire said.

"If what's true?" Lina asked.

"Nothing." Claire hurried away.

"What is with these people?" Lina asked.

Holly glanced at the cafeteria line and said, "Look out, Lina. Here comes trouble."

Lina looked up. Autumn exited the line with her tray. She started toward her usual table, where her friends Rebecca, Claire, and Ingrid were sitting. But she changed course and detoured to Lina's table. "Hi, Lina," she said. "Read my blog lately?"

Lina stiffened. Now what? What had Autumn done to her this time? Lina hadn't even had a chance to try to retaliate for the last one yet.

"No," Lina said. "Should I?"

"I think so," Autumn said. "It's always good reading. But the latest posting will mean a lot to you." She smiled and walked away with her chin jutting out.

"I'm afraid to look," Lina said.

"We might as well get it over with," Mads said. "Let's hit the library."

Nuclear Autumn: Keeping You Informed of the Latest Developments in the Lives of Autumn Nelson, Peter, and Tess

I'll come right to the point. You want your news and you want it now. So here it is: Many people admire our dear, sweet friend Tess's tresses. Some girls would kill for smooth, straight, shiny black hair like hers. But guess what: it's a wig! And if you want proof, just try tugging on it. I promise you it will come right off. Go ahead, pull her hair. It won't hurt her, because it's a wig. Don't be shy. She's a good sport. She'll think it's funny.

"Oh, my god." Lina's hands flew to her head as if she were about to be attacked by vicious hair-pullers right then and there. "No wonder everyone's been acting so weird. She's telling people to pull my hair!"

"The way her mind works is absolutely diabolical," Mads said.

Lina glanced around the library, afraid that someone might sneak up behind her.

"Don't let her make you paranoid," Mads said.

"Come on, let's get out of here." Holly took Lina by the arm. "I think I've got a hat in my locker. You can wear it to fend off the advancing hordes of hair-pullers."

"One sec," Lina said, typing something into the computer. "I've got something to do first." Autumn was going to get it now. That morning Ramona had written a sample anti-Autumn smear for Lina to post. Lina had thought it was too mean. But that was then, and this was now. Lina posted Ramona's fake story without changing a word.

Mood Swing
Current Mood: Hair-sensitive

Maybe you've heard—or maybe you haven't (I think the school is trying to cover it up) of the recent rash of thefts from the boys' locker room? Someone has been stealing the boys' shoes while they're busy at gym or sports practice. It looks like an inside job. School officials are baffled.

I think I can help them out. If you want to know where the stolen shoes are, check a certain girl's locker. You all know her. Let's call her "Summer."

Summer is very secretive about her locker. She doesn't like people to see inside. For good reason: She's hiding the stolen shoes in there. She is the shoe thief. Not only that, the back wall of her locker is plastered with pictures of men's feet. Snapshots, pictures cut from magazines, Odor-Eaters ads . . .

Why does she do it? Some people are just weird, I guess. You might call it a foot fetish. Normally this would be none of my business, but since there's a crime involved, and scores of innocent, unsuspecting boys are missing their favorite shoes, I thought it my duty to go public with this information. Summer, if you know what's good for you, turn yourself in. Otherwise, I'll have to.

As for all you boys, if you want to get Summer's attention, try waving your bare feet at her. The smellier the better. She won't be able to resist!

"How can you believe anything on that stupid Mood Swing?" Autumn screeched through the hallway later that afternoon. Rebecca trailed after her. Lina and Ramona pressed themselves against a locker, hoping Autumn wouldn't notice them. "It's all bullshit! And I've told you a thousand times, I'm not Summer!"

"But I saw you with David, and he had his shoes off," Rebecca cried. "You were ogling his feet! At least, I think you were. And I'm pretty sure I saw a whole bunch of pictures of shoes in your room one day."

Lina glanced at Ramona and suppressed a giggle. Thanks to the power of suggestion, Rebecca was actually imagining she'd seen the things Lina had put into her mind.

"They were women's shoes, and my mother put them there as suggestions for what she wanted me to wear to her wedding," Autumn said. "I don't get it—you believe Lina's blog, but you don't believe mine? Why aren't you tearing that wig off her head right now?"

"Claire tried, and it didn't come off," Rebecca said. "Because it's not a wig. Your blog is the one that can't be trusted."

They swept past Lina and Ramona, so caught up in their fight that they didn't notice the two girls retreating against the lockers. Still arguing, Rebecca and Autumn disappeared around a corner.

"This blog thing is finally paying off," Ramona said, clearly excited. "Let's get together later to plan your next posting. The shoe fetish thing was good, but now I'm thinking something along the lines of personal hygiene . . . ."

"I don't know," Lina said. "I think we've done enough to hold her for a while." Lina felt a little dizzy. "I've got to go to the bathroom."

She left Ramona and pushed open the door of the nearest girls' bathroom. It was empty except for a pair of feet in one stall. Lina turned on the tap and splashed cold water on her face. She heard sniffling. Then more sniffling. She leaned down to see whose feet were under the door, and immediately recognized Autumn's red wedge espadrilles.

Another sob. "Autumn?" Lina asked. "Are you all right?"

"Leave me alone," Autumn croaked.

"What's the matter?"

"Nothing," Autumn said. She started crying in earnest now.

Lina dried her face with a paper towel. She didn't know what to do next. How could she just walk out when Autumn was crying?

"Autumn, listen," Lina said. "I'm really sorry about everything. This blog war has gone crazy."

"How could you write such nasty things about me?" Autumn said. "What did I do to deserve it?"

Lina could think of several things Autumn had done, but it seemed mean to remind her of them now.

"Now Rebecca hates me, and all my friends think I'm creepy, because of the lies YOU wrote," Autumn said. She sobbed some more.

Lina felt terrible. She didn't like to hurt people.

"Listen, Autumn," Lina said. "I'm sick of this, too. It's all going to stop. I won't write about you anymore. Unless you want me to. I'll even write on my blog that I made up all those stories about Summer—if you'll do the same for me on your blog. Okay? Is it a deal?"

"You'll really do that?" Autumn said. "You promise?"

"I promise," Lina said. "Feel better now?"

"Yes," Autumn said. "Thanks, Lina. I'm so relieved that it's all over at last."

"So am I," Lina said.

18 Notes on Kissing

HERE IS TODAY'S HOROSCOPE: VIRGO: Other people may say you're okay, but you know in your gut you're a screwup. And as they say on *Oprah*: Always go with your gut.

What's his dog's name again?" Quintana asked.

"Nietzsche," Mads said. "NEE-cheh. After a German philosopher."

It was drizzly outside, so Mads and Quintana were spending a free period in the school library, reading magazines in the low reading chairs at the round magazine table. Mads was telling Quintana about her Stephen-kissing problem.

"So Stephen's into that stuff?" Quintana asked. "German philosophy?"

Mads nodded. "He's very smart and kind of serious, but also fun, you know?"

"He's still a boy," Quintana said. "Just remember that. No matter how intellectual they seem, deep down, they're all alike." She tossed a magazine on the table and reached for another one, stretching lazily like a cat.

"Hi, Quintana." The bulky form of Barton Mitchell loomed over them. "I tried to call you last night. Did your mother tell you?"

"Yes, she did." Quintana beamed up at him. He took this as an invitation to sit down in the chair next to her. "Sorry I didn't call you back. I was out."

"That's cool," Barton said. "I just wanted to make sure we're still on for Friday night. We are, right?"

"Friday night? I thought it was Saturday," Quintana said. Mads watched and listened, fascinated. This was the third boy to come talk to Quintana since she'd sat down half an hour ago. She'd toyed with every single one of them. She could make their emotions go up and down like a yo-yo.

Barton's face fell. "Saturday? I'm sure we said Friday. But I can see you Saturday instead, if that's better for you. I'll just skip my parents' anniversary dinner—"

Quintana laughed in her low, sexy voice. "Don't do that. I'm kidding. Friday night's cool."

"Yeah. All right." The clouds broke, and peace was restored to Barton's face. "See you then. Maybe I'll call you later."

"Okay," Quintana said. He got up and left. "I hope my mother didn't tell him I was out with Mo when he called last night. She has such a big mouth, and he gets so jealous."

"I don't think he knew," Mads said. She admired Quintana's power, but she felt sorry for Barton, too. Mads was a veteran of unrequited crushes. They could be painful.

"I've been training her not to blab," Quintana said.

"How do you do it?" Mads asked. "How do you keep them all so into you?"

Quintana waved the question away. "It's so not hard. I don't even know how to explain it."

"Well, do you have any kissing advice for me?" Mads said. "I can't figure out what the problem is with Stephen. I check my breath all the time, and it's always fine."

"What kind of gum do you chew?" Quintana asked.

"Gum? I don't usually chew gum."

"So how do you keep your breath fresh?" Quintana asked.

Mads shrugged.

"Maybe it's not as fresh as you think. Try wintergreen gum. If a guy takes me out for something to eat, I always chew some afterward."

"I like peppermint," Mads said.

"No, no! It has to be wintergreen. That's the strongest flavor. Plus, I read a survey in *Cosmo* that said guys like the taste of wintergreen better than fruit or peppermint flavors. By almost two to one."

"Really?" Mads pulled her geometry notebook out of her bag and jotted this down in the margin, even though she knew she wouldn't forget. "What else?"

"What are you doing with your hands while you're kissing him?"

"My hands?" Mads tried to think. "Mostly I'm just hoping they won't get in the way."

Quintana shook her head. "Put one hand on his back, and one on the back of his head. Then tilt your head slightly to the right. It's the best angle for them when they come in for the kill. And run your fingers through his hair while he's kissing you. They love that."

Tilt head right, fingers through hair . . . Mads furiously scribbled notes. This was priceless Quintana advice. How could the other girls not like her? She was so helpful!

"You can use both hands on the back of his head, too, if you want," Quintana added. "And if you get tired of mouth-kissing, you can kiss other parts of his face, for a kind of rest period. I can't believe you don't know this, Mads. Don't you ever watch movies?"

Watch movies for tips, Mads wrote. "Sure, I do," she said. "I just never realized they could be training films."

"What kind of gum is that?" Stephen asked. They were settled in his mother's studio again. Mads had made sure that Nietzsche had plenty of food and water in the kitchen.

"Wintergreen," Mads said. "Want some?"

"No thanks," Stephen said. "It smells good, though."

Score one for Quintana, Mads thought. She tilted her head to the right, practicing. To get ready for what she hoped was coming next.

"What are you doing?" Stephen asked, mirroring her head tilt with one of his own.

She straightened her head. "Nothing. I have a crick in my neck."

"You do?" He put his hand on the back of her neck. "Want me to rub it for you?"

"That would be great," Mads said.

She relaxed as he rubbed her neck. It felt good even though there really was no crick. She stopped chewing her gum, letting it rest under her tongue. She glanced around the immediate vicinity, looking for a good place to stash it when the time came. An ashtray, a cup, anything . . .

Stephen rubbed her neck more firmly, and soon he had his other arm around her, his face close to hers. She put one arm on his back and one on his head, as Quintana had instructed. She tilted her head a little to the right. She closed her eyes.

He kissed her very softly. She opened her eyes to see if his were closed. They were. She closed hers again and moved the hand on his back up to his neck. She ran her fingers through his hair. He sighed and pressed her down on the couch, kissing her more deeply now.

Yay, Quintana, Mads thought. This was more like it.

He eased the pressure on her lips. She remembered what Quintana had said about kissing other parts of his face, so she playfully nipped at his nose. He smiled. She kissed his cheek, then his forehead, then nibbled a strand of his hair. . . .

Stephen lifted his head to look into her eyes. But Mads' eyes were drawn higher, to his forehead. Dangling from his bangs was a gooey white lump. Her wintergreen gum.

"What's wrong?" Stephen pulled away and sat up. The wet gum flapped against his forehead. His hand flew up and touched it.

"What is it?" he asked.

"Hold still," she said. "It's only gum." She gave it a little tug, hoping it would peel right off. But there was hair wrapped around it. Lots of hair.

"Ow! Careful. How stuck is it?" he asked.

She didn't want to say. But she'd seen gum casualties like this before. Gruesome.

"I'm afraid we're going to have to amputate," she said.

Stephen stood up and went to a mirror on the studio wall. He stared at the gum in distress. "You mean, cut it out? Right in the middle of my bangs?"

"It won't look so bad," Mads said. "We'll just snip the bottom part. You'll still have all your bangs. They'll just be shorter in the middle."

"But that will look extremely stupid," Stephen complained.

Mads bit her lip. She couldn't argue with that.

"What if we cut all your bangs shorter, so they're even," she suggested. "A Caesar cut."

"I hate Caesar cuts," Stephen said. "Only dickweeds have Caesar cuts."

Mads knew he was upset because she had never heard him use the word "dickweed" before. It wasn't his style.

She'd screwed up again. Whenever she tried to do something Quintana's way, it backfired. Now she'd ruined

Stephen's hair. He was going to look like a dickweed and it was all her fault.

"Maybe, on you, a Caesar cut will look classic, and not dickweedish at all," she said. "Since you're not a dickweed, you can't look like one."

He turned away from the mirror. "Aw, Mads, don't get upset. I bet my mother can fix it. She's pretty good with scissors." The sticky hair stuck straight out from his forehead. Mads tried not to laugh. Laughing at him would only make things worse.

"I'm really sorry," she said, and she was. Sorry about ruining his hair. Sorry that there probably wouldn't be any more kissing that night. Sorry that she was the biggest makeout screwup since the beginning of time.

19 Sebastiano's Crystal Ball

To:	hollygolitely
From:	your daily horoscope

HERE IS TODAY'S HOROSCOPE: CAPRICORN: Feeling lost? Why are you surprised? You're taking spiritual advice from a computer!

I have a date with Eli tonight," Holly said. She settled on the red velvet couch next to Sebastiano for another episode of *Los Días del Corazón*.

The Altman-Pecks lived in a rambling, low-ceilinged, stucco bungalow furnished with an eclectic array of antiques and decorated with portraits of Sebastiano's relatives and ancestors. Sebastiano identified a few of the subjects of the larger portraits: "That's Great Aunt Millie"—a 1920s flapper covered in furs and bugle beads. "She was married eight times—once to a Vanderbilt. And, over there, that's Uncle Harvey, the inventor of Tidy-Blue Toilet Bowl Cleaner."

"Cool," Holly said. She'd always wondered what Sebastiano's house was like. Somehow she'd pictured him in someplace airier, less cluttered. An ancient Venetian palazzo, maybe, filled with modern Italian furniture and portraits of dukes on the walls.

"Yes, much of this was paid for by the Tidy-Blue bonanza," Sebastiano said. "That, and a little windfall from Taste-Rite Denture Cream."

He brought her an orange seltzer and set a plate of turkey, cheese, and crackers on the coffee table.

"Where are you going on your date tonight?" he asked.

"I don't know yet. Eli's going to tell me later."

"After he sees what Otavio is up to, you mean," Sebastiano said.

"I suppose," Holly said. "I hope Otavio is in the mood for mushroom pizza today. I'm getting a little tired of *mole poblano*."

"Let's activate our crystal ball and see." Sebastiano clicked on the TV.

[Translated from Spanish]

"Where are we going?" Marisol shouts over the wind. She and Otavio are speeding down a winding seaside road on a motorcycle at night. The moon shines on the water. Marisol holds his waist tightly.

Otavio's square jaw twitches. "We are going to find our destiny," he says. Marisol looks nervous.

The motorcycle stops at a rocky, deserted beach. Otavio dismounts and helps Marisol. In spite of the moonlight, the water is churning and dark.

Marisol: Take me home. You know I'm afraid of the ocean.

Otavio: You must not be afraid. Come with me into the water.

He takes off his shirt and flexes his super-cut muscles.

Marisol: No.

Otavio: But the night is warm. All day I've been dreaming of a midnight swim with you. Come. Don't you trust me?

Marisol looks warily at the waves crashing on the shore.

Otavio: I won't let anything hurt you. Please— trust me.

He reaches for her hand. Close-up on Marisol's face. She looks terrified.

(Commercial.)

"Can you believe this guy's bod?" Sebastiano said, chewing on a thin slice of cheese. "He must work out six hours a day."

"Why is Marisol so afraid of the ocean?" Holly asked.

"Um, I think her mother drowned in the ocean when she was a little girl. After being drugged by her third husband, Marisol's stepfather. Who was then convicted of second-degree murder. They showed it in a flashback a while ago. The stepfather is about to be let out of jail soon, which is also making her nervous."

The show came back on.

The terror on Marisol's face softens. She slips her hand out of Otavio's grasp. He looks angry. But then she pulls her chiffon dress over her head. Naked, she gives Otavio her hand and together they run into the waves. They splash and dive happily.

Marisol: My fear is gone! I'm liberated! I feel so free. Thank you, Otavio.

Otavio: I'll take my payment now.

He kisses her hard as the waves crash over

them. They roll around in the surf. They are obviously about to make love. Otavio pauses in their passionate kissing.

Otavio: This was a test, Marisol. I needed to know that you trust me. Now our fate is sealed. I know it is our destiny to be together.

Marisol: Yes. Our fate is sealed. I am yours, Otavio.

(Fade out.)

"Woo!" Sebastiano said, slapping Holly on the thigh. "You're in for a hot time tonight!"

Holly couldn't help it—while dressing for her date, she found herself drawn to her blue flowered silk chiffon with the ruffle at the neck. She caught herself reaching for it, then slapped her own hand away. "No! Stop it!" she scolded herself. It was the closest thing she had to the dress Marisol had worn on the show that day. Holly didn't want to fall into that trap, copying Marisol just because Eli was copying Otavio. But it was hard to resist. The evening was especially warm, and the chiffon seemed perfect. In the end, she gave up and wore it. Maybe I should try to be as much like Marisol as I can, she thought. She was curious: What would Eli try to pull that night? How far would he really go?

She pinned her hair up in a loose bun, the way Marisol sometimes wore it, but that was too much. She undid her hair and let it hang straight down her back.

There's no way he can re-create the show exactly, Holly thought. They didn't live far from the beach, but the water was too chilly for swimming, and, anyway, Holly had no fear of the ocean, so what would be the point? Still, she gave her bikini a glance, wondering if she should stuff it into her bag, just in case. On second thought, no. If she did, he might suspect that she was onto him. And she wasn't ready to let him know that yet. As long as he didn't know that she knew his secret, she still had power over him.

I'll just go along on this one last date, she thought. Just to see what he pulls this time. I'll have a little fun with him, like Sebastiano says. Then she'd dump him. And it would be a total shock. The girl dumping the guy was not in Eli's script.

Eli picked her up at seven. He looked pleased with her dress. He was wearing jeans and a flannel shirt, different from Otavio's flashy clothes, but then, it was practically a boy uniform. There were probably dozens of guys in Carlton Bay wearing the exact same thing that very night. And, to her relief, he was still driving his Honda Civic and not a motorcycle.

"You look beautiful, as always," Eli said as she got into the car. "Let's just go for a ride."

They zipped through town to the Marina, a bayside area full of cafés, restaurants, ice-cream stands, and shops. Eli parked and they walked along the boardwalk, holding hands. Holly found herself glancing warily at the water where the boats were docked. It didn't look all that clean. "What do you want to do?" she asked.

"I was thinking maybe some fried oysters from Zola's," Eli said. "Do you like oysters?"

"Love them," Holly said.

They went to Zola's take-out window and ordered fried oysters, French fries, and iced teas. When their food was ready they settled on a bench and watched the people stroll by. The boardwalk was busy; it was a beautiful, warm Friday night.

Holly dipped an oyster in tartar sauce. "Mmmm . . . these are so good."

"Yeah." Eli grinned at her. He had a little tartar sauce above his lip. Holly wiped it off with her napkin.

"It's warm tonight," Eli said. "Almost summer-hot."

"Maybe it's all the lights," Holly said. The boardwalk was well-lit at night. Moths swarmed the old-fashioned gas lamps that lined it.

"You know what would be great?" Eli dumped his paper plate in the trash and wiped his hands on a napkin.

"What?"

"To go for a swim. A midnight swim." He put his arm around her. "Wouldn't that be romantic?"

Holly froze, her fork halfway to her open mouth. He was really doing it. This was just like the show!

I can't believe this guy, she thought. He was actually sticking to his script. This was almost too easy.

"But it's only nine o'clock," she said.

"Okay, then—how about a nine-thirty swim?"

Patience, patience, she told herself. *Don't show your hand yet.* "But where can we swim? The ocean's too cold."

Eli flashed her a wicked grin. "Leave it to me. I think I know the perfect place."

Oh, please, she thought. *Spare me the melodrama.* But she couldn't help wondering what the perfect place would be. If not the ocean . . . where?

Eli drove inland and out of town. Holly found herself in a suburban area of office parks and malls. It was late at night, and the malls were closed. Everything was deserted. He pulled the Honda into a dark parking lot and cut the lights. Holly could barely make out the sign: ACTIONLAND WATER PARK.

"Why are we stopping here?" she asked.

"Don't you want to go for a swim?"

"Here?" Through a chain-link fence Holly could see a

large waterslide. It wasn't really a whole water park, just a single slide. The fence was padlocked, the park was dark, and Holly could only assume that the water wasn't running.

"Where else?" Eli said. "Don't worry—we won't get caught. There's nobody around for miles."

"But—" Holly had so many objections, she hardly knew where to begin.

"Hey," Eli said. "Take a chance. It will be fun. Come on—don't you trust me?"

He got out of the car. She stayed where she was. He opened her door and gave her his hand. He helped her out.

"I didn't bring a suit," she said.

"We'll go in our underwear. You *are* wearing underwear, aren't you?"

Holly blushed. Yes, thank god, she was wearing underwear.

"Come on, then!" He flashed that mischievous grin again, and she was charmed in spite of herself.

"I don't understand," she said as she followed after him. "How—?"

He climbed the chain-link fence. It wasn't too high. She stuck a sandaled foot into one hole of the fence and hoisted herself up, careful not to catch her skirt on the metal. He caught her on the way down. They were in the park. It was dark, except for the moonlight and a street-lamp in the parking lot.

The giant slide loomed over them, dark and dry. "There's no water," she said.

Eli went to a small shack and picked the lock. "Don't worry, I've done this before."

"You have?"

"Run the slide, I mean. My uncle owns this place. I worked here last summer."

"Oh." Holly relaxed a little. At least if they were breaking and entering it was on his uncle's property. Maybe, if the police came, the uncle wouldn't press charges. That would be a plus.

In the shack, Eli turned on a light and started the water system. Holly heard water stream down the slide with a hiss.

Eli took her hand. "Woo-hoo! Let's go!"

She followed him up the plastic stairs to the top of the slide. "I can't believe we're doing this," she said. She turned to look at the landscape around her: the red and white lights of the few cars on the highway; the dark, empty parking lots dotted with security lights; the barren suburban shopping zone. It was nothing like the beautiful Mexican beach where Otavio and Marisol had their tryst.

But the two places had one thing in common. From high above, a three-quarter moon shined its pale beams down upon her. "This is so weird. Like a moonscape."

He took off his shirt and pants and stood before her in his underwear. Plaid boxers. She liked them. He took both her hands in his. "Are you nervous?"

"A little," she said.

"Don't be afraid. You can trust me."

And she did trust him, for the first time. She was finally getting a glimpse of the real Eli. Not a dashing Otavio clone, but a normal guy. A guy whose uncle owned a water park.

Just like Marisol, she took off her flowered dress. *A bra and panties are the same as a bikini*, she told herself. *Or almost the same. Nothing to be embarrassed about. Nothing he hasn't seen a million times before on the beach.*

"Nice bikini," he said, grinning and waggling his eyebrows at her.

"Keep your eyes on the slide," she said.

Hand in hand, in their underwear, they stood at the edge of the slide. "You ready?"

"Ready," she said.

He said, "One, two, three, go!" And down they plunged.

20 Ramona's Expertise Goes to Waste

To:	linaonme
From:	your daily horoscope

HERE IS TODAY'S HOROSCOPE: CANCER: They say let a smile be your umbrella, but with a smile like yours, that's a good way to get wet.

Mood Swing
Current Mood: Peace-loving

News of the day: Autumn Nelson, author of the delightful Nuclear Autumn blog, was seen sharing her post-lunch brownie with her friend Claire today. How sweet! She can be so generous. Some might say that her true motive was cutting her dessert calories in half, but the fact remains that she shared her brownie.

Bravo, Autumn! I would also like to add that her chestnut hair looked particularly lustrous today. What's your secret, Autumn?

"I don't understand," Ramona said. "She was mean to you. She's brilliant at it. Why did you write those nice things about her? Are you setting a trap? Is it some kind of joke?"

"I decided to be the mature one and stop the madness," Lina said.

Ramona looked blank. "Why?"

"I felt sorry for her," Lina said. "Writing mean things about her wasn't working, anyway. So I changed tactics."

"You call this a tactic?" Ramona said. "Praising her hair?"

"I'm killing her with kindness. Anyway, I want to be a real journalist," Lina said. "Not a tabloid gossip writer. So I only wrote true things. True, nice things. As much as I could stomach. It wasn't easy to find something to say, believe me. If I'm being nice and she's being mean, it makes her look bad. She won't be able to keep trashing me much longer."

"I'm disappointed in you, Ozu. You had so much potential. You were a talented reputation trasher. Under my expert tutelage, you could have gone far." Ramona sighed. "But I guess you don't have the guts for it. Shame, really."

"You'll see," Lina said. "By the end of the week, Autumn will be on her knees. She'll be saying nice things about 'Tess,' and the war will be over. And my chances of getting the internship will rise because I will be able to demonstrate my journalistic integrity to Erica."

Ramona stared at her. "You're serious, aren't you."

Nuclear Autumn: Keeping You Informed of the Latest Developments in the Lives of Autumn Nelson, Peter, and Tess

Tess has dog breath. Why do you think Peter won't kiss her anymore? Pass it on.

"See?" Ramona said. "I told you it wouldn't work."

"But look how lame her posting was," Lina said. "Three sentences! She's losing strength, I'm telling you."

Dear Autumn,
Why are you still writing about Peter and Tess or Lina and
  Walker or whoever they are? Your last posting on them
  sucked. We want to hear more about YOUR life, your
  greedy stepmonster-in-waiting and annoying half sister
  and clueless dad. Bring back the news of Autumn!
—An anonymous fan

Dear Anonymous,

Finally somebody has some brains around here! I totally agree
that Tess/Lina and Pete/Walker are huge bores and
nobody cares about them. Why bother with their snooze
news?

Dad's girlfriend, Chloe, is way more heinous than anybody at
RSAGE could ever be. I haven't written about her in a
while, so we have a lot to catch up on. First: Dad bought
her a beautiful diamond tennis bracelet for her birthday.
He was so excited to give it to her and he thought she
was going to be thrilled. But she wasn't. She called it
"ordinary." She demanded that he take it back to Cartier
and exchange it for a bracelet with rubies, emeralds,
and sapphires because "color is in right now." Of
course, the ruby, etc., bracelet costs like ten times more
than the diamond one, but poor Dad coughed up the
money, thus depriving me and my college fund of
another few thou. . . .

"That was you, wasn't it?" Lina said to Ramona. "The
anonymous fan?"

"It was time to put Tess and Peter out of their misery,"
Ramona said. "Can we all please move on now?"

"Thanks," Lina said. Peter and Tess were finally dead.
Lina and Walker were very relieved. That night she
pressed on Walker's squeaky spot to celebrate.

21 The Tongue Rule

Is it me? Is it him? What am I doing wrong?" Mads asked Quintana. They were sitting on the bleachers after school, watching the boys' varsity lacrosse team practice.

"Tell me again what happened," Quintana said. "And this time, give me every single detail."

"The gum thing was kind of a fluke," Mads said. "The main problem is, whenever we're really into it, and I start to French-kiss him, something interrupts us. It's getting to the point where I think I'm turning him off. But, why? He seems really eager to kiss me at first, but—"

"Stop right there." Quintana shook her head in disapproval. "Did you say *you* start to French-kiss him?"

"Yes?" Mads said uncertainly. "What?"

"No, no, no," Quintana said. "Mads, don't you know about the Tongue Rule?"

The Tongue Rule? "I've never heard of that," Mads said.

"I thought everybody knew it," Quintana said. "The Tongue Rule is: Never put your tongue in a boy's mouth first. Always let *him* do it first."

"But why?" Mads asked, baffled. This sounded like a rule left over from her grandmother's days, like expecting a boy to stand up when you entered a room. Remnants from another time. Another one that was big with Grandma: "No boy will ever want to marry you if you don't learn to hold a fork properly."

"It's one of those weird boy-secrets," Quintana said. "If you go first, it makes them feel like they don't have control. It scares them. Maybe when they're older and have more confidence it's okay, but with high school boys you must always follow the Tongue Rule."

"All this time I've been violating the Tongue Rule without realizing it," Mads said. "No wonder Stephen's been so weird with me. How can I reverse the damage?"

"Just start following the rule now," Quintana said. "It's not irreversible. Things will get better soon, Mads, if you let him take the lead."

Mads sighed. So she *had* been doing everything wrong. But why did she have to let the boy take the lead? It was very frustrating. She didn't like to wait. She wanted to take charge and make things go in the direction *she* wanted.

Well, she decided, if it would make Stephen more comfortable, it was worth it.

On the field, a whistle blew. The lacrosse ball got away from one of the players and rolled toward the girls, stopping at Quintana's feet. Mads waited for Quintana to pick it up and toss it back onto the field. But Quintana just leaned back, shook her long hair, and tapped the ball with her toe.

A boy—Mads couldn't tell who it was because he had his helmet on—ran over to the sidelines and called, "Little help?"

Why was Quintana just sitting there? Mads leaned forward to reach for the ball and throw it back on the field.

But Quintana stopped Mads' hand. "Wait," she said. "Sit back."

Mads sat back. The boy crossed the sideline to scoop

up the ball with his stick. Two other boys ran off the field, racing to get to the ball first. Inches away from Mads and Quintana, they battled over the little white ball at their feet, knocking helmets and slapping at each other with their sticks. Finally, one of the boys trapped the ball, scooped it up, and cradled it in the netting. He barked out a victorious laugh and glanced back at the girls—the winner! The other boys wouldn't give up, kept clacking their sticks against his, trying to knock the ball away.

The coach blew his whistle. "Quit fooling around over there. Back to the scrimmage!"

"Thanks for the help, girls," the boy with the ball said, a flirtatious lilt in his voice.

"Did you see that?" Quintana said. "They weren't fighting over the ball. They were fighting over *us.*"

"They were?" How did Quintana know these things? She seemed to be reading a secret code that Mads didn't even know was there.

"Trust me. They were," Quintana said.

"Did one of them win us?" Mads asked.

"No," Quintana said. "Because we're not that easily impressed."

"Oh." *I still have a lot to learn*, Mads realized with a pang. Her ignorance of boys was overwhelming. Scary. *So much to learn.*

22 Betrayal

HERE IS TODAY'S HOROSCOPE: CAPRICORN: After you die, your ghost will haunt the earth like one of those losers who keeps coming back to high school after graduation. Why am I telling you this now? Just to see the look on your face.

Otavio—dressed in pressed jeans, a pink polo shirt, gold chains around his neck, a yellow sweater tied rakishly over his shoulders, tasseled loafers, no socks, and hair freshly blow-dried—answers the door of his lavish villa. At the threshold stands Blanca, Marisol's beautiful blond younger sister. She is dressed in a tight, brightly colored, cleavage-enhancing wrap dress and red spike heels.

Otavio: Blanca!

Blanca: Otavio—I have to talk to you. May I come in?

Otavio (letting her in): Is everything all right?

Blanca: No. It's Adolfo. (She looks shaken.)

Otavio: Adolfo! Your adopted brother?

Blanca (sobs): Yes. Oh, Otavio, it was horrible! (She throws herself into his arms. As he holds her, the camera reveals a sneaky look on her face that Otavio can't see.)

Otavio: What did he do to you?

Blanca: He tried to . . . he tried to . . . kiss me, and then . . . (dissolves into tears)

Otavio: My poor, darling girl. (Looks at her, then kisses her. She returns his kiss, passionately.) Oh, Blanca.

Blanca: Oh, Otavio!

(They stumble into Otavio's bedroom, all over each other, and fall into bed.)

Otavio: Wait, my darling. I have to make a quick call first. (He reaches for his bedside telephone and dials a number he knows well.) Marisol? Darling, it's me. I have bad news. I can't make our dinner date tonight. I'm sorry, beloved, but it's business and I can't put it off. I'll call you later. Love you. Kiss kiss.

(He hangs up and snuggles up beside Blanca in bed.)

Otavio: Now, where were we?

(Commercial.)

"That was hot," Sebastiano said.

"I found it disturbing," Holly said.

So far, Otavio had only had eyes for Marisol. And that was how Eli had behaved, too. Now, all of a sudden, Otavio was a giant cad? Now that Holly was falling again for Eli? How could those Mexican writers change the script on her this way?

"Disturbing?" Sebastiano said. "Why? Would Eli seduce your sister?"

"I doubt it, since she's in college and not exactly interested in high school boys," Holly said.

"So? You're safe."

"Not necessarily," Holly said. "The point is that Otavio is cheating on Marisol. Does that mean Eli will cheat on me?"

"Are you seeing him tonight?"

"Yes," Holly said. "We're going out to dinner." *It's just a TV show,* she told herself. *Don't freak.* But she knew Eli would take it and tweak it in his own special way. The question was, how would he do it?

Her cell phone jingled. Holly looked at the caller ID. Eli. "It's him," she said.

"Oh, my god." Sebastiano slid across the couch to be closer to the phone.

"Hello?" Holly said.

"Hey, it's me," Eli said. "Listen, I can't make dinner tonight. I'm really sorry. I promise I'll make it up to you."

Holly froze. This was unbelievable. "What's the problem?"

"Nothing big, just family stuff. I'll call you later."

"All right." Holly clicked off. She turned to Sebastiano. This was too weird.

"Look at it this way," Sebastiano said. "He doesn't do *everything* like Otavio. He doesn't wear those heavy gold chains, or tasseled loafers without socks. Or tie his sweaters around his neck. He doesn't, does he?"

"How do I know?" Holly asked. "Maybe, in the privacy of his room, he secretly does all that and more. Maybe he even irons his jeans. What kind of guy patterns his whole life on a soap opera?"

"A lunatic?" Sebastiano said.

Holly frowned. "That's what I was afraid you were going to say."

23 Cletus the Slack-Jawed Yokel

To:	mad4u
From:	your daily horoscope

HERE IS TODAY'S HOROSCOPE: VIRGO: A question will be answered, but it's not the one you asked.

"It happened again," Mads told Quintana. Mads was glad to find her in the lunchroom Thursday morning, having coffee before classes began. Quintana: her guru, her adviser, her savior. Mads mixed herself a hot chocolate and sat down. Rebecca and Claire walked in and waved to them from the coffee station. Quintana waved back. It looked as if things had warmed up between Quintana and the female population of RSAGE.

"This time, I followed the Tongue Rule," Mads said. "I held it in check. Then he started French-kissing me. His tongue was all over the place. So I figured it was okay to release Old Sloppy and let her do her thing."

"What happened?"

"The same as always," Mads said. "He bolted upright, as if I'd stuck him with a pin, and that was it. Makeout session over."

Quintana tore open a sugar packet and stirred it into her coffee. She shook her head. "Mads," she said. "I have to confess something. My store of boy knowledge has never been so tested. I've run out of advice."

"You have?" Quintana run out of boy advice? Had Mads tapped her dry?

"Almost," Quintana said. "I have one last piece of advice for you. If this doesn't work, you're on your own."

"What?" Mads asked, impatient for Quintana's last gem. "What is it?"

"Talk to Stephen," Quintana said. "Ask him what's going on."

"Ask him?" Mads was disappointed. This was the kind of advice her mother would give her. But she'd tried everything else. It was the only choice left.

"What if he shuts down?" Mads asked. "What if he won't answer me?"

Quintana shrugged. "Then you'll have to keep wondering."

"That would suck," Mads said.

"That's the chance you take," Quintana said.

After another aborted make-out session in his mother's studio—Mads thought she'd give him one last chance—Mads dropped the charade and confronted Stephen.

"Stephen," she said. "Can I ask you something?" She leaned her right shoulder into his side and played with the buttons on his shirt with her left hand. She wanted to make sure he knew she wasn't complaining, exactly, but just curious. "Have you ever noticed . . . anything funny . . . about the way we kiss?"

"Funny?" He puckered up and kissed her quickly on the lips. "No. I like it."

"I like it, too," Mads said. "I love kissing you. That's why it bothers me—or, I wonder why—it always has to stop so . . . abruptly? Before we really get anywhere?"

"What do you mean?" he asked, but she saw something flicker across his face. He knew exactly what she meant. Something was up, she was sure of it.

"I mean, I'm getting into it, and suddenly you stop," Mads said. "Quintana told me I was breaking the Tongue Rule—"

"What's the Tongue Rule?" Stephen asked.

"You should always let a boy initiate French-kissing," Mads explained. "Or they freak out or something. But last time, you started Frenching me, so I thought it was okay for me to do it. But you stopped me."

"That's crazy," Stephen said. "Your friend Quintana doesn't know what she's talking about."

"Then what is it?" Mads asked. "Is something wrong with me? Does my mouth taste funny? Is my tongue too rough? Do I turn you off somehow?"

"Mads, no!" Stephen hugged her and kissed her and hugged her harder. "Nothing's wrong with you at all! You're so cute and very sexy and you always taste like delicious fruits or mints."

"Then what is it?" Mads asked. "I don't understand."

He hesitated. "It's kind of embarrassing."

"That's okay," Mads said. "I won't make fun of you."

He squirmed. "It's—it happens when you put your tongue in my mouth."

"I'm doing something wrong, aren't I," Mads said. "I knew it. I just don't get French-kissing!"

"No, Mads, you kiss great," Stephen said. "I like that little swirly thing you do. It's not that. It's . . . This is so embarrassing . . ."

"What? You can tell me."

"Well . . . look." He opened his mouth wide. Mads peered inside. She saw a tongue, teeth, fillings . . .

"What? Do you pick up radio waves through your fillings or something?"

"No." He pointed toward a spot in the back. "I'm missing a tooth. In the back. One of my molars. See that gaping hole?"

Gaping hole? "Oh, yeah," Mads said. "But it's not a gaping hole. It's just a little tooth-sized empty spot."

"It feels huge to me," Stephen said. "And I can see it sometimes, if I look in the mirror and smile really wide or open my mouth as if I'm laughing."

Boys checked themselves out in the mirror that way, too?

"But what does that have to do with kissing?" Mads asked.

"I was afraid you'd feel the hole with your tongue and get grossed out," Stephen said. "I was afraid you'd laugh at me. I feel like a toothless hick. Like Cletus the Slack-Jawed Yokel."

This did make Mads laugh. "You mean like the guy in the joke who's so inbred, he's his own grandpa? Just because you're missing a little tooth?"

"See?" Stephen said. "You're laughing."

"I'm laughing at the joke you made, not at you," Mads

said. "I never even noticed that silly hole. Relax. You don't have to worry about it—I swear. Even if I feel it, I promise it won't gross me out. Unless there are chewed-up crumbs stuck in there or something."

"I always brush before I see you," Stephen said.

"Then there's no problem," Mads said.

"Really?"

"Really." To prove it, she kissed him, flicking the missing tooth spot with her tongue. "Mmm, what a delicious gaping hole," she whispered. "Nothing turns me on like a missing tooth."

"Glad you like it." They kissed some more. Stephen peeled down one strap of her tank top, letting it flop over her upper arm. Underneath, her new camisole showed. He admired it, playing with the strap.

"Where did you get this?" he asked.

"Quintana took me lingerie shopping," Mads said. "It's a camisole. We bought a thong, too, but"—she hesitated, remembering the broken thong nightmare—"but it didn't work out."

"Well, Quintana might be wrong about French-kissing," Stephen said. "She's probably wrong about a lot of things. But there's one thing she got right: This little camisole is very sexy on you."

"Glad you like it, Cletus," Mads said.

She kissed him again, brazenly flaunting the Tongue Rule. Stephen didn't stop her. They kissed and kissed late into the night, so late that Mads almost missed her curfew. Which was exactly as it should be.

24 Otavio, How Could You?

To:	hollygolitely
From:	your daily horoscope

HERE IS TODAY'S HOROSCOPE: CAPRICORN: You're in the mood to stay up late and sleep in. It's always darkest before the dawn, and why would you want to see the mess you've made in broad daylight?

Have you heard from Eli?" Sebastiano asked.

"Not since he called to break our date on Friday," Holly said. "I have no idea what's going on." Sebastiano and Holly had come to his house after school Monday for the next installment of *Los Días del Corazón*. Holly was a little nervous. She didn't like the notion that her fate was being determined by a bunch of

TV writers in Mexico. She'd gone along with this bizarre setup out of curiosity, and then, to get back at him, and because it was kind of fun. Along the way, she'd somehow let herself fall for Eli more than she'd meant to. She regretted it now. Big mistake.

Sebastiano fixed her some chamomile tea to calm her down. He offered to raid his mother's medicine cabinet for a sedative, but Holly refused. If she needed to take a sedative to watch a soap opera, things had really gone downhill.

Sebastiano turned on the TV. "You know what I wish Otavio would do today?" Holly said. "Come clean to Marisol. Tell her everything. Explain what he's thinking."

"I doubt that will happen," Sebastiano said. "It's not very dramatic."

"He could at least tell her he's sleeping with her sister," Holly said.

Otavio is getting out of bed with Blanca. She wears one of his shirts. He is dressing. He kisses Blanca, preparing to leave.

Otavio: I have to go meet that pig, Marisol.

Blanca: But, why? Stay here with me.

Otavio: Don't worry, darling. It will all be over soon.

Holly gripped Sebastiano's hand. This was not looking good.

> Marisol waits for Otavio at a fancy restaurant. He is late, but she's not too worried. She innocently believes that he is busy with his work. Otavio strolls in and kisses her.
> Otavio: I'm sorry I'm late. The world of drug-dealing and international crime doesn't stop for dinner.
> Marisol: I understand, my love.
> Otavio sits down at the table. He orders a Scotch and downs it quickly.
> Marisol: Is something wrong, Otavio?
> Otavio: Marisol. This is not easy for me to say. I don't want to hurt you. But I must be honest.

"Honest?" Holly said. "He's never honest. Why does he have to be honest now?"

"Keep cool, Holly," Sebastiano said. "We don't know what will happen yet. You know how these shows are, full of twists and surprises and sudden, brutal murders. . . ."

> Otavio: Marisol, I must leave you.
> Marisol (stricken): What?

Otavio: I love another. We must part. We shall never make love again.

Marisol (weeping): But, why? Who is this other that you love?

Otavio: I cannot say. Please don't take it so hard. I'm sorry, but I must go now. (He leaves the restaurant.)

Marisol collapses, sobbing. Cut to the beach, where she and Otavio once made love. Where she lost her fear of the sea, because of him. Marisol reaches into her bag and takes out a big bottle of pills. The label says sleeping pills. She pours them down her throat, chasing them with vodka. Then she walks grimly into the ocean.

(Commercial.)

"He dumped her!" Holly cried. "I can't believe he dumped her."

"Drowning herself in the ocean," Sebastiano said. "That's how her mother died. Love the symmetry." He paused. "And all because of Otavio. I wonder if anybody would ever kill themselves over me?"

Holly slumped against the back of the couch. "Is Eli going to follow through with this? Will he really break up with me now, after all we've been through—just because of this stupid show?"

"How should I know?" Sebastiano said. "Are you going to go out with him again?"

"I might as well," Holly said. "I have to see this story all the way to the finish."

"But you already know how it ends."

"I guess," Holly said, but she had a flicker of doubt. Her thoughts flashed to a moment on the waterslide, the two of them in their underwear, and Eli's hand in hers. That Eli, the real Eli, wouldn't dump her. He wasn't slick like Otavio.

This was Eli's last chance. She saw a tiny ray of hope. It was Eli versus Otavio. Which one would win?

25 A Diary with a Lock on It

To:	linaonme
From:	your daily horoscope

HERE IS TODAY'S HOROSCOPE: CANCER: You know that saying, "Be careful what you wish for, because you may get it?" Well, don't worry—you're not going to get it.

Did you hear about the internship yet?" Walker asked. He and Lina were lounging in a hammock in his backyard. It was early Friday evening and getting cool and dark out, but Walker kept her warm. The light from the kitchen window made her feel safe as they lay together and listened to the frogs and the crickets.

"Yes," Lina said. His hand was resting on her stomach,

and she absently played with his fingers. "I didn't get it. Neither did Autumn. Nobody at RSAGE got it. I think they gave it to a Griffith kid."

"Did Erica say why?"

"Yes." The memory of Erica's phone call that afternoon was fresh and still a little painful. "She said she enjoyed Mood Swing and Nuclear Autumn. She found them very entertaining and was kind of sorry to see the gossip die down. She even said she thought my writing was good. But she was looking for investigative reporting skills. And Mood Swing definitely wasn't about that."

"No, it wasn't," Walker said.

"And my sports clips from *The Seer* didn't help me there, either," Lina said. "Sports writing is not investigative reporting. I guess I was hoping she'd be so impressed with my writing skills, it would override that. I was wrong."

Walker squeezed her hand. "You'll get another summer internship—something better. You *are* a good writer. And you're only a sophomore."

"I know," Lina said. "I still feel like kind of a loser, though, letting Autumn get me all caught up in her insanity." She reached down, where her slouchy leather bag sat half-open on the ground, and rummaged around inside it. "Look what I got." She showed him a small blue hardcover book with a lock on it and a key dangling from a loop. "It's a diary," she said. "To write my thoughts and memories in. I've already written my first entry. I got one with a lock for maximum security."

"Good thinking," Walker said. "No need to share every intimate moment with the world." He reached for the diary. "Let me see that."

"Walker!" She snatched it away and hid it under her legs. "It's private!"

"I just want to see if there's anything about me in it," he teased, grabbing for the book. "I won't tell anyone what you wrote." He started tickling her. "You'll have to let go sometime. . . ."

"No!" She wrapped her body around the book and tried to shield herself from his fingers. They tumbled out of the hammock to the grass. The diary fell about a foot away from where they landed.

"I'm going to get it!" Walker said, but instead of going for the diary he went for Lina. They rolled around on the grass, laughing.

26 Eli vs. Otavio

To:	hollygolitely
From:	your daily horoscope

HERE IS TODAY'S HOROSCOPE: CAPRICORN: You will hear the words "evil twin" today. Yes. Every single person born under the sign of Capricorn will hear those words today. It's one of those astrological flukes.

I t's so good to see you tonight," Eli said. He reached across the table at Le Mas, a romantic restaurant just outside of town, and touched her hand. Holly wondered why he'd bothered to bring her to such a nice place only to dump her. But, then, that's what Otavio had done to Marisol.

"I'm sorry I had to cancel our last date," Eli said. "I felt really bad about it." He stared into her eyes.

Holly sensed an ax hanging over her head. It made her bold. "Why did you cancel? You never really told me."

"It was . . . it was totally unexpected," Eli said. "There was . . . a crisis . . . and I had to deal with it. A family crisis. I think I told you that."

Holly just nodded, waiting for more. Not that his family crises were any of her business. But he owed her a better explanation than that.

"See—" he stammered, "I just found out I have a twin. An evil twin. A long-lost, evil twin. He showed up out of nowhere, threatening to blackmail my mother because she abandoned him. It was a real shock."

"A long-lost, evil twin?" Holly rested her chin on her hand and raised an eyebrow. She didn't have the energy for this anymore. "That *is* a shock."

"Well, yeah. My mother was a wreck. And I was in no shape to go out."

"Where is he now, this evil twin?"

"I don't know," Eli said. "He made his threat, then he left. He said he'll be in touch with us later about how much money he wants to keep quiet. So—you know—don't tell anybody about this or anything. It's kind of a secret."

"Don't worry. Nobody would believe me if I told them, anyway."

He laughed nervously. "Ha. That's for sure."

Their appetizers arrived. They ate in silence. *Why don't you just get it over with?* she thought. *If you're going to dump me, dump me!*

But he didn't. They finished their appetizers, ate their entrées, and ordered dessert. And he still didn't dump her. It was odd. Otavio had dumped Marisol before she'd had a chance to order a drink.

"Is something bothering you?" Eli asked. "Are you upset that I canceled our date?"

"No," Holly said.

"Because sometimes things come up," Eli said. "When your life is crazy like mine. The world of drug-dealing and international crime doesn't stop for dinner."

Holly stiffened. She knew that line. It was one of Otavio's excuses for standing up Marisol. Eli was grinning, making a joke out of it. But it felt like a slap in the face.

"I understand, my love," Holly said, pointedly, in a Mexican accent. "*Mi amor.*"

Now he looked stricken. He dropped his fork. "What did you say?"

Holly pressed on. "Our fate is sealed. I am yours . . . Otavio."

"Oh, my god," Eli said. "You know."

"I've been watching every day for a couple of weeks

now," Holly confessed. "I know you do everything Otavio does. So why don't you just get it over with and dump me already?"

"Dump you? Why would I do that?"

"Because Otavio did it. On the show. But, believe me, I'm not going to swallow a bottle of pills and try to drown myself. I hope you won't be disappointed that I'm not following the script. I'll be fine. You don't have to worry about me."

Eli shifted in his chair. He looked down at his lap, wiped his mouth with his napkin, and put it on the table. Holly could read his thoughts on his face. He was trying to decide what to do next.

"Okay, I confess," he said. "I've been copying Otavio. The first words I said to you came from him. But it's only because he's so cool. He's such a stud. Girls will do anything he wants."

"Your motives are so noble," Holly said.

"I know it sounds bad," Eli said. "I'm never sure what to say or do around a girl I like. But when I pretend to be Otavio, I always know what to do. He hands me great lines to say—and they work. It worked on you, for a while."

"Please. I'm humiliated enough."

"Don't be! I'm the one who's embarrassed," Eli said. "I

only did it because I really like you. I wanted to impress you. I was afraid you wouldn't like me if I was just plain old Eli Collins. I wanted to be exciting."

"But you've been lying to me!" Holly said. "And you did break our last date, and your evil-twin excuse is not cutting it."

"All right, I'll tell you the truth," Eli said. "Maybe then you'll see why I lied. The real reason I broke our date was because it was my little sister's birthday. I'd forgotten about it. Her party was the night of our date. My parents got mad at me when they heard I was going out. They wanted me to go with them to Chuck E. Cheese and help them supervise the twelve screaming brats my sister calls her friends. Happy now?"

Holly laughed. "Chuck E. Cheese? That's almost as unbelievable as a long-lost, evil twin."

"It's not as cool," Eli said. "I was afraid you'd think I was a geek."

"Maybe I would have, but I'd still like you," Holly said. "I wanted to get to know you, the real you. It's pretty impossible if everything you tell me is a lie. Didn't you worry that I'd figure it out eventually?"

"I tried not to think that far ahead," Eli said. "But yeah." He wiped his mouth again. "Look, Holly. I don't care what Otavio did to Marisol. I don't want to break up with you. I want to keep seeing you."

Holly looked into his gray, labyrinth eyes and realized that, in spite of everything, she still liked him. A lot.

"Will you?" he asked. "Keep seeing me? If you don't mind dating a soap opera addict."

"I don't mind," Holly said. "I'm becoming one myself."

He leaned across the table. She met him halfway. They kissed. It was good. And now she finally had the answer to his mystery. Or one of them.

"Are you sure you don't want to break up with me?" Holly asked. "I have a sister you can fool around with, you know."

"I'm sure," Eli said. "From now on I'm writing my own script. And it says right here"—he pointed to his hand as if it held a piece of paper—"it says here that we should kiss some more. A lot more."

"Okay." She kissed him on the lips. "But I reserve the right to ad lib, when I want to." She kissed him again. "And to cut all references to long-lost, evil twins."

"Just keep kissing me."

She did. They knocked over a glass of water, and she hardly noticed.

A question floated through her mind: *Can you find true love in six minutes?* She still didn't know. The answer was: Maybe. But she was leaning toward Yes.

Parallel Parking

Sean led Holly to the dance floor. They danced for one song, and then dinner was served. Holly went back to her table.

"Dancing with Sean—how'd that happen?" Lina whispered to her.

"Did Mads notice?" Holly asked.

"She was in the bathroom with me," Lina said. "I walked back in here first, saw you on the dance floor, and turned Mads back around, saying she had crab in her teeth."

Holly nodded. But she thought it was a little silly that Mads had to be protected from seeing her dance with Sean. It was just a dance. It didn't mean anything.

Still, for the rest of the night, Holly found herself catching Sean's eye from across the room. They didn't dance together again, or say anything to each other. But whenever she looked at him, he was looking at her.

"I'm ready to go," Holly said to Sebastiano toward the

end of the evening. "Do you need a ride?" Walker and Stephen were going to take Lina and Mads home, so Holly would be driving home by herself.

"Sure," Sebastiano said. "Let me just say good-bye to a few people."

"Okay," Holly said. "I'll meet you out by the car."

Outside, Holly found Sean leaning against her car.

"Heading home?" he said.

"Yep," Holly said. She put her key in the door. Sean took her by the elbow.

"Hey," he said. "I really like you."

Startled, she turned toward him and looked up. He kissed her. When she'd recovered, Holly glanced around. Did anyone see that? Did Mads? People all around were getting into their cars, but no one seemed to have noticed Sean and Holly.

"What are you doing tomorrow night?" Sean asked.

Holly frankly couldn't remember if she had plans or not. "I don't know . . . ."

"Want to go do something?" he asked.

She needed a moment to take this in. Was Sean Benedetto asking her out? Looked that way. She was curious to find out more about him. But Mads' face loomed in her mind. What would she think if Holly went out with Sean, her eternal crush, her personal rock star?